THE DALAI LAMA'S CAT AND

THE CLAW

OF

ATTRACTION

ALSO BY DAVID MICHIE

THE DALAI LAMA'S CAT AND

THE CLAW

OF

ATTRACTION

DAVID MICHIE

CONCH
CONCH BOOKS

First published in 2023

CONCH

Conch Books, an imprint of Mosaic Reputation Management (Pty) Ltd

Cover design: Sue Campbell Book Design
Cataloguing-in-Publication details are available from the National
Library of Australia www.trove.nla.gov.au

ISBN 978-0-6458531-0-0 (print)
ISBN 978-0-6458531-1-7 (e-book)

HOMAGE

With heartfelt gratitude to my precious gurus:
Les Sheehy, extraordinary source of inspiration and wisdom;
Geshe Acharya Thubten Loden, peerless master and
embodiment of the Dharma; and
Zasep Tulku Rinpoche, precious Vajra Acharya and yogi.

Guru is Buddha, Guru is Dharma, Guru is Sangha,
Guru is the source of all happiness.
To all gurus I prostrate, make offerings and go for refuge.

May this book carry waves of inspiration from my own gurus
To the hearts and minds of countless living beings.

May all beings have happiness and the true causes of happiness.
May all beings be free from suffering and the true causes
of suffering;
May all beings never be parted from the happiness that is
without suffering, the great joy of nirvana liberation; and
May all beings abide in peace and equanimity, their minds free
from attachment and aversion, and free from indifference.

PROLOGUE

How can I describe the vehicle that was driving slowly across the courtyard of Namgyal Monastery? Like none I had ever seen before, dear reader. Extremely long – three times the length of a regular sedan car – it was a great, gleaming hulk, somewhat military in appearance, but colored hot pink. Like a spaceship from another planet.

Plenty of heads were turning. These included the usual mix of tourists who'd come to photograph the splendor of the monastery temple, set against the soaring, ice-capped Himalayas. Monks making their way to and from their nearby residence. Traders at their gate-side kiosks, selling all manner of food and drink to passers-by. All of them stopped and gaped at a vehicle that seemed designed to grab attention, as it slowly rolled to a halt.

No movement was evident behind the darkly tinted windows. Then a door opened and there was an eruption of laughter, as ten glamorous young women came tottering out in high heels, arms extended as every step was accompanied by a flurry of selfies. Group selfies. Individual selfies. Selfies juxtaposing the temple roof and looming mountains, at just the right angle to showcase a sparkling piece of merchandise – a handbag, bracelet or some make-up item – alongside their brightly beaming faces.

"This is all so spiritual!" they cooed as they glanced around, relishing the attention of onlookers.

After the initial jolt of surprise, things in the courtyard began returning to normal. Namgyal Monastery may be tucked far away in the Himalaya foothills, but being the home of the Dalai Lama, people here are quite used to extraordinary visitors. The most recent arrivals were taking it in turns to be photographed at the front of the limo, its dazzling fuchsia color in giddying contrast to the muted gold of the temple and icy transcendence of the mountain peaks.

Not everyone, however, was indifferent to the new visitors. Returning from a meeting at the monastery, the moment His Holiness caught sight of the pink apparition, he pointed towards it and burst out laughing. Accompanied by two bodyguards and a huddle of monks, he wasn't visible to onlookers as he steered his group towards the vehicle, curious to inspect it more closely. I was following in his footsteps, a short distance behind.

Approaching from the back of the vehicle, His Holiness reached out with childlike curiosity to tap the gleaming bodywork with his knuckles. To study the glistening reflective glass of the tinted windows. On the far side of the car from the young women, he caught sight of them gathering, their backs towards him, preparing for a group photo. A mischievous twinkle appeared on his face.

Edging further up on the other side of the car, the Dalai Lama stepped out from behind, just as the chauffeur, acting as photographer, counted down: "Three! Two! One!". It was a classic photobomb, dear reader! The chauffeur was the first to react with laughter and amazement. The young women were turning. Recognizing who it was, they screeched with excitement before clamoring towards him.

His Holiness's bodyguards – huge humorless warriors, always on the lookout for a security breach – had soon closed around him, wanting to verify the identity of the visitors. The fashionably dressed occupants of the hot pink carriage were quick to brag that they were none other than India's Top Ten Social Influencers Under 30, with a combined online audience of over one hundred million followers. They were on a three-day tour of the Himalayas.

"Social influencers?" mused the Dalai Lama, meeting their exultant eyes as soon as his security detail stepped aside. They were zeroing in on this unanticipated and truly sensational photo op.

A tall dark-eyed beauty in a crimson dress was waving her gold clutch bag excitedly. "You know," she wanted to make sure he understood, "Instagram. Digital media."

"Yes, yes," said the Dalai Lama. "Lots of friends like this," he mimicked, scrolling on an imaginary device.

"You see!" They were enraptured.

"Tell me," His Holiness reached out to gather the hand of crimson girl on his left side, and that of a young woman in a lemon-yellow sari on his right. "What do you use your influence among this hundred million people to do?"

"To sell stuff!" Crimson girl laughed, brandishing her clutch bag, showing off the distinctive interlinked gold letters of a well-known luxury brand.

A woman directly in front of the Dalai Lama in emerald green gazed at him, as if the two of them already had a deep, shared understanding and knew better than this. "I help women discover their sacred sexuality," she brought a hand to her heart. "To attract love into their lives."

If His Holiness was in any way surprised by this intimate revelation, he gave no sign of it.

To his right, yellow sari woman was determined to have her say. "I show people ..." she raised her voice shrilly above the rising clamor, "that they can be whatever they want to be!"

The women were vying for the Dalai Lama's attention like the raucous teenagers that some of them still were. Crowing about how influential they were. Seeking advice. Wishing to take selfies to share with their millions of followers – as fast as possible! The noise level quickly rising, during the hubbub one of them cried out, "Let's ask him how to manifest stuff!" as if he wasn't even there.

There was a new surge of gleeful babble before a feisty young woman in shimmering sapphire shoved emerald-green girl forcefully to one side as she stepped before him, brought her palms theatrically to her forehead and bowed very deeply. "Your Spiritual Highness, please teach us about the law of attraction."

The noise level receded as he regarded her with benevolent amusement. "The law of attraction?"

"You must know it!" One of them was calling from the ruck.

"How to manifest things in your life," sapphire girl was

explaining. "By affirmations. Getting the universe on board to create abundance."

"Oh, I see!" His Holiness chuckled, exchanging a glance with Oliver, one of his Executive Assistants who was accompanying him. The two sometimes discussed the curious ways in which Eastern ideas were packaged as pseudo-spiritual commodities, by Westerners seeking to make their fortunes.

The Dalai Lama met sapphire girl's blazing eyes with a compassionate expression.

"In Buddhism, we say that reality is all mind's creation."

"Yes, yes!" she nodded fervently.

"The way we are experiencing things right now is only arising because of our minds," he was looking at the young women's attentive faces. "And each of us is experiencing a somewhat different reality."

"So how can we experience a reality with the new diamante sunglasses …" crimson girl named a designer label, "which are so hard to come by?"

"Or the perfect boyfriend?" Emerald-green was pushing back.

"Or your ten millionth online follower?" Yellow sari wanted to know.

The Dalai Lama regarded their flushed, animated faces, his forehead wrinkling. "This materialist approach," he nodded, "seeking to change what you believe to be entirely outside you. It has many problems. For example, why must you constantly postpone your happiness?"

India's Top Ten Social Influencers Under 30 were taken

aback by this question. Staring at him, their eyes filled with consternation. Postponing happiness was something they most definitely wanted no part of.

"For example, if our happiness depends on having the new diamante sunglasses," he chuckled. "Or the perfect boyfriend," he beamed from the crimson girl to the emerald-green one. "Or having ten million followers," he nodded at yellow sari. "What do we do until then? If we are constantly yearning for material things that we don't have, then our happiness is always around the corner. Or at the top of the next mountain. Why do you not wish to be happy here and now? Without needing anything else. Happy as I am?"

As always when he spoke, His Holiness communicated with more than words alone, so that he also conveyed an experience of what the words meant – with inescapable significance. His audience was quite mesmerized.

"Moreover," His Holiness held up his forefinger emphatically. "How long do we get happiness from the new sunglasses? The new partner? The tenth millionth follower? A few weeks? Perhaps months? And then," he smiled at emerald-green girl, "no more honeymoon! Perhaps there are new sunglasses from another designer and the old ones are out of date?"

Something was shifting among His Holiness's audience. It was as if he were giving voice to a truth they had already experienced, but hadn't been able – or perhaps willing – to face. In just a few sentences, he had quietly demolished the entire basis of a reality they'd never questioned. Gone was all the giggling and the fake bravado. The swagger and the contrived poses. Now they were just a group of young women, open and unaffected, hanging on his every word.

"Influence is power," he continued, his expression thoughtful. "And power can be very dangerous if not used carefully. For example, we may create envy among others by parading the things we have." He was studiously avoiding looking at any of them in particular. "If our followers feel they are missing out on the good fortune we have, we may cause them pain. This is unfortunate. It is the opposite of the true cause of happiness, which is to give happiness to others. And it is a karmic cause for us to suffer the same kind of pain in the future."

Some of the women were looking at the ground. Tears were welling in the eyes of others. But the young woman in the yellow sari wasn't so easily swayed. "Are you saying we should give up on our hopes and dreams?" she asked, voice choked with emotion.

"No, my dear," the Dalai Lama turned to her, shaking his head decisively, "that's not what I am saying. Worldly ambitions, especially when you are young, can be motivating. Useful. But we must see them for what they are. It is wonderful to enjoy mundane pleasures when we have them," he nodded towards the stretch pink vehicle with a chortle. "But ultimately, such things are not really so important, so meaningful." As he shrugged, a sense of non-attachment to worldly things felt as palpable as the mountain breeze that was gusting across the courtyard. And his words as self-evident. "Better," he observed, "to be ambitious in other ways."

The women began to huddle, seeking comfort in one

another from the challenging shift in perspective delivered so gently but with such undeniable consequence. Emerald-green and sapphire girls, looking down, met each other's eyes and reached out to one another. The others followed, unguided and spontaneous. In the next few moments, they formed a circle of joined hands, connecting to each other – and to His Holiness.

"In what way should we be ambitious?" Crimson girl asked.

The Dalai Lama smiled. "We should all wish, very much, to develop our hearts and minds," he told them, the radiance of his expression lifting their faces so that, one by one, each of them was meeting his eyes again.

"When we see that all other sentient beings are truly just like us, that we all wish for happiness and we all want to avoid suffering, then our own love and compassion quite naturally arise. Sometimes," he tilted his head musingly, "when we open our hearts, the most remarkable surprises can occur."

With His Holiness's words resonating, I decided that this was my moment. Slipping among the legs of several monks standing behind him, I rubbed myself against his legs, before taking my place in the middle of the circle of young women, looking up at them.

"The Dalai Lama's Cat!" Several gasped in amazement.

"She really exists!"

"Absolutely beautiful!"

I took in their youthful, wonderstruck faces, recognizing that whatever luxuries they had known as India's Top Ten Social Influencers Under 30, whatever incredible extravagances they had experienced, none of it compared to this simple moment, here and now, standing in the courtyard of Namgyal Monastery with the Dalai Lama – and the Dalai Lama's Cat.

Across the circle, there was a question that sapphire girl just had to ask. "If the law of attraction isn't about getting things, or relationships, what is it to attract?"

His Holiness was nodding. "It is to attract the inner qualities we need for transformation. Virtues such as equanimity, authentic loving kindness, wisdom. When we train our minds correctly, we abandon the tiny view we usually have of ourselves as mere bags of bones seeking this thing or that, and become aware that our real destiny is as fully enlightened beings."

The young women beheld him transfixed. Awe-struck by his pronouncement. And yet at the same time – perhaps because of his presence – the alternative ideal of themselves as awakened *bodhisattvas* seemed not only desirable, but achievable too.

"Where to begin?" Crimson girl asked ardently.

"Are there any Buddhist secrets?" Sapphire girl wanted to know.

"We begin," the Dalai Lama spoke clearly, "when we have a strong wish to turn away from constant dissatisfaction. When we recognize the limits of worldly activity. On that basis," he looked over at sapphire girl, "we engage in the practices of *bodhichitta* and *shunyata*. When these are perfected, our job is done."

The truth of his words was as radiant and all-embracing as the charge that surged through the circle. For a few moments, the power of his inspiration caught them all up in a state of transcendence as real as the courtyard where they stood, the temple and the towering mountains in the distance – even the bright, pink limo nearby.

Reaching my front paws before me, I stretched out in a luxuriant sun salutation. Given my advanced years, it was a creakier version than when I was younger. And because my life had become somewhat more sedentary, my talons were longer and more pronounced as they extended from my paws.

"Those claws!" exclaimed sapphire girl.

"The claw of attraction!" chimed yellow sari and everyone burst out laughing.

"Never forget this teaching," His Holiness twinkled. "About the claw of attraction!"

Bodyguards were stepping between him and the young women on either side, slipping their hands apart with the smoothness of practice, and guiding the Dalai Lama to his next appointment.

"That was …" Crimson girl was shaking her head, moments after he had gone. "There are no words."

"I'll never be the same!" declared emerald-green effusively.

For the longest time they stood in uncustomary silence, trying to absorb what had just happened. Then, fully stretched, I began following in His Holiness's steps.

And as I left, I heard yellow sari observe ruefully, "We didn't even get selfies!"

CHAPTER ONE

WHEN IT COMES TO FOOD, THERE IS NOTHING THAT WE CATS like more than novelty. The beguiling aroma of some unexpected morsel rising from one's bowl. The intriguing flavor on sinking one's fangs into a new and flavorsome treat.

That morning Tenzin had arrived to serve breakfast, His Holiness being away on a visit to Sera Monastery. From his satchel he produced a brand of cat food I had never seen before. On disgorging its contents into a saucer, a pungent tang of seafood instantly filled the room.

"There you go, HHC!" Tenzin always addressed me with a certain formality, using the initials by which I was known in official circles, an abbreviation of His Holiness's Cat. He placed the saucer on the floor in front of me, with an expression that rarely crossed the face of such a consummate diplomat. He wasn't even trying to hide his revulsion. Had I been able

1

to speak, I might have passed on the Dalai Lama's frequent reminder that nothing is inherently pleasant or unpleasant from its own side. It is merely your karma that forces you to see it as so.

Had I been able to speak, however – even if for this one and only time in my life – I wouldn't have. As soon as the saucer touched the floor my face was in it, inhaling the ripe and unusual deliciousness as I took my first, noisy mouthful.

"A medley of cod, sole and shrimp," Tenzin was reading aloud from the packet above me, "presented in a lavish, briny sauce."

Quite why he should find this of interest, I neither knew nor cared. The succulent scrumptiousness of the food was all that preoccupied me.

Food has been my constant obsession from the time that I first arrived in Dharamsala as a tiny kitten. And one person understood my cravings better than anyone. That morning, dozing in a room which felt empty and forlorn without the Dalai Lama's presence, my thoughts turned to her quite naturally. To the treats and morsels that she constantly bestowed on me. The effusive welcome I was always guaranteed. High time, was it not, to visit His Holiness's VIP Chef, Mrs. Trinci?

Until recently, such a visit wouldn't have been possible – she lived too far away. As I padded out the gates of Namgyal Monastery, I recalled the unexpected and quite enchanting discovery that had brought my number one fan within my ambit.

Mrs. Trinci's daughter Serena and her husband Sid lived

only a short distance away at 21 Tara Crescent. Further up the same road as Namgyal, they had a raised, rambling bungalow with white walls and a spacious wraparound veranda, its most distinctive feature being a crenellated tower that rose up two stories and was shrouded in ivy. Near the top was a room with wide picture windows on all four sides – a viewing chamber in which I had passed many an evening, taking in the spectacular vistas and communing with the sun, the moon and the ice-peaked Himalayas ranged far above and behind the house.

In the time they had lived there, Sid and Serena had made numerous renovations to their home, before the arrival of their first child, Rishi, nearly three years earlier. Because it was such a large block of land, its terraced lawns leading to pine forests stretching far into the distance, they were continually unearthing new aspects about the property.

One such revelation had occurred on an afternoon last summer. Serena had decided to take Rishi for a picnic somewhere they'd never sat before, on the far boundary of the garden. Vast bushes of crimson and purple bougainvillea marked the end of the terraced lawns and the beginning of the forest. Or at least, they seemed to.

Sid had emerged from the house to join them. No sooner settled, he received a business call. Getting up to talk, he circumambulated the dazzling tangle of bougainvillea. Which was when he noticed something. Urging Serena to come take a look as soon as he ended the call, within moments she had joined him behind the unruly profusion. Ahead of them lay a stretch of flat ground, recently turned over. At the end of it, twenty yards away but before the forest began, rose a magnificent and singular tree all on its own.

"An Italian umbrella pine!" Serena had exclaimed, eyes gleaming. "Just like in Ravello!"

Mrs. Trinci had often talked of retiring to Ravello, high above her beloved Amalfi Coast. It was a fanciful dream of course, her own life and that of her daughter's being far too well-established in McLeod Ganj to seriously contemplate such a change.

But in nostalgic moments, especially over a glass of Chianti or Vermentino, her dark eyelashes would flutter closed as she described the sublime vistas of her childhood: the wide, unruffled cobalt of the Mediterranean rolling towards infinity. The languid gold light of summer evenings, heavy with lavender and a choir of cicadas. And soaring upwards, like coastline sentinels, Italian stone pines, their vast canopies offering sanctuary from the heat and the rain, their branches always a-whisper with secrets immemorial.

"But I love my trees!" she would wail, if Serena was ever too heavy-handed in suggesting permanent retirement in McLeod Ganj.

"What about my trees?" she would dare those who suggested it was pure sentiment that still attached her to the old country.

The trees in question were Italian umbrella pines, *pinus pinea*, for which she'd had a fervent affinity since childhood. And now, unexpectedly revealed here in McLeod Ganj, a most imposing example, lofty and distinctive.

Sid told Serena that he'd recently asked the gardener to clear the patch behind the bougainvillea of the dense thicket of vegetation that had taken root there. And how the removal had for the first time exposed, in all its towering glory, the tree beyond. Serena walked right up to it, mesmerized, before turning to face Sid. Which was when a fresh brightness lit her face.

"Do you know what this is?" she'd asked, with some excitement.

"What?"

"Come and look from here!"

Walking over, Sid stood beside her, turning towards the bougainvillea. Like Serena, he noted a symmetry that wasn't obvious from the other end. Rhododendrons stretched tall on either side of the newly cleared ground. A hint of sandstones marked the borders of onetime flowerbeds. Closer by and strewn with leaves, a small, paved area. A moss-filled dip.

"This used to be a garden!" surmised Serena.

Astonished, Sid strode purposefully towards the mound of bougainvillea. He crouched, peering inside the thicket, shoving away its thorny branches. "And if I'm not mistaken," he turned back to her, "this pile of rubble was once a cottage. Small. Just a couple of rooms."

She joined him, pushing back strands of flowers to look beyond. It didn't take them long to find the remnants of a wall. "A beautiful cottage could be rebuilt right here," mused Sid. "We already have the established garden. The pine tree, just like Ravello."

"Are you thinking what I'm thinking?" Serena's eyes were alight.

"How could I not?" Sid shrugged, with the enigmatic air of the maharajah that he was. "It's written in the stars."

WITHIN A DAY OF SERENA AND SID'S DISCOVERY, MRS. TRINCI had visited to inspect the rediscovered garden for herself. Venturing behind the bougainvillea. Surveying the emerging borders of mature rhododendrons. Most extraordinary of all, marveling at the stately Italian umbrella pine, tears rising to her eyes as she approached, as though towards a much-loved and yearned-for friend with whom she was being reunited after decades. Putting her arms around the trunk, she had held there for the longest time, communing with a fellow compatriot who had also put down roots in this Himalayan village, so far away from home.

There and then the decision was made. Within weeks, plans for Mrs. Trinci's new cottage had been agreed, approved and a builder appointed. Because the project wasn't a major one, and because Sid was well-connected, it wasn't long before the new home was built. Small and simple, designed to her specifications, its open-plan living area and kitchen leading to a sitting room, then veranda, all facing onto the verdant lushness of a newly laid lawn. And at the far end, a centerpiece, upright, soaring, unmistakably Mediterranean, the guardian spirit of her new home.

For my own part, I had kept a keen eye on developments up the road, usually visiting the construction site at twilight when the hubbub had died down, taking in the strange, harsh scents of building materials. When needed, making use of the extensive sand piles. Over the weeks I had watched as foundations had been dug, walls emerged from the ground, then rafters and a roof appeared.

The time of greatest curiosity for me was after Mrs. Trinci had moved in. During the course of a single weekend, there was suddenly a whole new house of furniture to explore. And because Mrs. Trinci was my greatest benefactor after only the Dalai Lama himself, and frequently called me The Most Beautiful Creature Who Ever Lived, there was no question of my being able to explore it.

The afternoon of this particular visit, I headed down the side of the house as usual, entering through the sliding doors which led from sitting room to veranda. Mrs. Trinci would keep them open so that *prana* could circulate.

"Oh, *tesorina*! My little precious! You are also coming to tea?" Behind the glistening kitchen benches and wearing an apron, Mrs. Trinci was doing what she did best of all – preparing a delicious indulgence.

I chirruped. I had no idea about a tea gathering, but the aroma of baking that emerged from the oven was promising; whenever Mrs. Trinci treated her friends and loved ones, I was sure to be included.

Heading to the sofa closest to the kitchen, I hopped onto the seat, then arm, then back, where I could sit, watching her work her magic. Dark hair swept from her face in a bun, gold bracelets clashing noisily about her right arm as she moved; she was immersed in what she was doing.

I had been a regular observer of Mrs. Trinci my whole life, mostly in the kitchen at Namgyal where she prepared meals for the Dalai Lama's VIP guests. In the early days, she had been operatic, and on occasions, tumultuously volcanic. One of her conversations with the Dalai Lama, from my first days as a kitten, had been of special consequence. Having been invited upstairs by His Holiness after a most successful lunch with several United Nations delegates, Mrs. Trinci had seemed awkward, even reluctant to accept his thanks. When he had used the phrase 'loving kindness' when talking about her work, she had even objected.

"If only it was loving kindness, Your Holiness!" she had rebuffed him.

The Dalai Lama had regarded her with some surprise – as well as compassion. Raising both palms, he urged her to go on.

"I have listened to your teachings and read some *Dharma* books. There is much talk about the mind of infinite altruism. But I cannot lie, this is not my mind. If only it was!" Her eyes had widened as she regarded him woefully through dark, mascara lashes. "I live on my own. I do little to help others. I think mainly of myself. All day long!"

"But you work here," countered the Dalai Lama. "And in a voluntary capacity."

She shrugged.

"You give great happiness to my guests. And of course," he rubbed his tummy with a mischievous smile, "to me!"

Mrs. Trinci was ambivalent. "Sometimes, perhaps, you are being kind. Polite."

"But not this one," His Holiness gestured to where I was following the exchange, sprawled on the sill, an empty ramekin beside me. With a chuckle he added, "She doesn't pretend."

Mrs. Trinci's expression lightened. "True," she said.

His Holiness regarded her closely for a while before asking softly, "You do not think of what you do as practicing loving kindness?"

She shook her head.

"Not even when you are cooking for us?"

"I am too busy concentrating," she replied.

There was a long pause before he spoke again. "In that case, I have a formal request," he said, his gaze turning suddenly very serious. "From now on, I would like you to add a special ingredient to every meal."

Mrs. Trinci's expression was grave.

"*Bodhichitta*," he said. "You know it?"

"The wish to attain enlightenment for the benefit of all living beings," she quoted the definition.

He nodded. "By making this meal," he mimicked stirring a pot, "may all beings have delicious food. May their everyday needs be met. May they be free from suffering," he proposed.

"For the main course?" she queried.

"For *every* course," he replied. "*Every* action in the kitchen. Outside the kitchen too. As much as possible. Whenever you are able to think, recollect *bodhichitta*. The wish to attain enlightenment to free others from suffering."

A look of hesitation passed across Mrs. Trinci's face, as if she was about to say something, but thought better of it.

"What?" he met her eyes.

"*Bodhichitta* is all very well," she admitted after a while. "But just wishing for something won't make it so."

The faintest twinkle came into his eyes. "It will change what happens in *your* mind. You think only of yourself, you said? This is not a cause of happiness. But what happens when you think of helping others with kindness?"

She didn't need to reply. Already a rueful smile was appearing on her face.

"What happens if you train to keep thinking this way?"

"I suppose it becomes part of who you are."

"It changes who you are, yes? First the thought to help others. Then the action." The Dalai Lama smiled, reaching over to squeeze her hand. "Never forget the special ingredient."

Since then, Mrs. Trinci spent much of her time in the kitchen recollecting *bodhichitta*. She added the special ingredient to every course of every meal she cooked for His Holiness and his guests. To every batch of scones that she made for his staff. She incorporated it into the pots of tea she sent upstairs to the Executive Assistants' office, or brewed for Serena and herself, at work or home.

And over the years, she had become a less Wagnerian version of herself. It was as if those powerful surges of negative emotion had transmuted to positive ones, the compassionate energy that sometimes overtook her every bit as elemental as the displeasure once so forcefully on display.

Perched on the sofa, softly purring, I could tell she was adding the special ingredient right now. She was guiding dough from her bowl into a baking pan, lips moving very slightly and a particular expression coming over her face.

Just as His Holiness had said, not only had her *bodhichitta* become instinctive. She had come to focus on those around her with such compassionate attention that there were times when her very presence seemed to permeate the space around her with a benevolent sparkle, not much different from that of the Dalai Lama himself. She would always be Mrs. Trinci – demonstrative, bracelets clanging, larger than life. But as well as that, she had developed an open-heartedness, an impassioned generosity that drew people to her like bees to one of the extravagant bowers of rhododendrons running down the length of her rediscovered garden.

I can't, dear reader, claim that afternoon's archaeological discovery was entirely of my own making. That while exploring a well-established but long-hidden garden, it was I alone who had pushed through the unmapped undergrowth to make the most remarkable finding. The way it happened was like this.

At four o'clock precisely there was a knock on the front door, and Mrs. Trinci opened it to welcome the first of her guests, Serena, Sid and little Rishi. The moment Rishi saw me, he squealed with joy. Face alight, he rushed across the sitting room in my direction.

Something about his energy sent a jolt through my system. After a languorous afternoon, I found that I was suddenly frisky. Instead of waiting for him, I sprang up and raced outside. Rishi chortled, gleeful at the game. Paying no attention to his mother's warnings not to run too fast, he pursued me across the veranda and onto the new lawn.

I scampered down the garden in the direction of the tree. As he followed, arms outstretched, I zigzagged with gusto. He continued after me. We were running out of lawn space. I darted under the cover of the great green leaves of a Delicious Monster at the far corner of the garden.

Rishi dropped to all fours. He was about to continue the chase.

His mother had other ideas. "Rishi, no!" she cried.

Sid pounded down the lawn. "Not in the flower bed!"

The wrathfulness of her tone gave him pause.

As I ventured further into the darkness, Rishi was pushing back the leaves.

Sid had arrived and seized him. Rishi was still clutching a leaf. As he was raised up, it was as though he was tugging open a curtain – the deep shadows where I was sitting were momentarily a dazzle of sunlight. In that instant, the glitter of silver caught my eye.

It came from only a couple of feet away. When Rishi let go of the leaf and the darkness returned, I kept my gaze fixed on the spot. Had there really been something or was it only a play of light? I stepped over towards where it had come from and pawed the ground.

The earth was covered in dead leaves and decaying pine cones, empty snail shells, cobwebs and the detritus of garden undergrowth. Dipping my head, mouth open the better to catch every nuance of resinous odors, as I scuffed at the ground my paw struck something metallic. Dull and grey and about the size of a phone, it was lightweight, moving easily at my touch. I was sniffing at it when Serena pushed the leaves apart.

"Rinpoche!" she was already calling out when she caught sight of me. Then, curiously, "Rinpoche?" as she saw me pawing the object which was glinting once again. "What have you got?"

Looking up, I meowed.

She shuffled closer and reached through the leaves. "She's found something!" she called to the others who were standing on the veranda. Turning the discovery over in her hands, she dusted off decaying matter that was stuck to it. "Engraving," she mused as she returned up the lawn. "Some kind of plaque."

Coming out of the undergrowth, I followed her. Sid was distracting Rishi with a toy train. Serena and Mrs. Trinci had their heads together, scrutinizing the writing.

"Italian!" exclaimed Mrs. Trinci. "Look *la gatta prediletta* – the favorite cat!"

"*Requiescat in pace*," read Serena. "Latin."

The two women exchanged a look of astonishment, before their gaze turned inevitably towards where I approached them. Sid was soon there too.

"Here lie the … mortal remains of …" Serena replied to his expression of inquiry by translating slowly, rubbing at the metal and tilting it to better read the engraving.

"Luna," Mrs. Trinci got there first.

"Yes. Luna."

13

"The favorite cat of …"

"Something Lorenzo."

"Padre?"

Mrs. Trinci shot her daughter another electrified expression. "A priest?"

"Father Lorenzo," Serena nodded. Before adding, "Rest in peace."

"And the date?" asked Sid.

"14 February 1957."

At that moment, something happened to Mrs. Trinci that I'd never seen happen to her before. Nor was it anything I could ever have imagined happening to her. Clutching her hands to her heart, she fixed Serena with a thunderstruck expression.

Mrs. Trinci, dear reader, was rendered speechless.

Serena drew her mother into her embrace. Facing Sid, she said, "That's the year Mum was born."

Sid raised his eyebrows.

"Meanwhile," he said, "a Catholic priest had already discovered this little part of paradise in the Himalayas, and was living in this very place with his beloved cat …"

"And the tree," Mrs. Trinci managed at Serena's shoulder.

As the women broke apart, Serena smiled. "Yes. And the umbrella pine he must have brought to remind him of home."

Mrs. Trinci was shaking her head, eyes glistening as she absorbed the revelation.

"To think," Serena looked from Sid to her mother, "we had no idea about any of this when we moved here."

"And still wouldn't," emotion tugged at Mrs. Trinci's mouth as she spoke, "if it hadn't been for little HHC."

As one, the humans turned to look at me with great fondness of regard, the kind – was it wrong of me to think like this? – I found most promising, given that afternoon tea was about to be served.

Two other guests arrived within minutes: Dorothy Cartright, one of Mrs. Trinci's closest friends, a similar vintage to herself and quintessentially British, and Binita, the widowed friend of Serena and Sid's who had come to Dharamshala to manage Sukhavati Spa. An elegant woman in her early forties, with smooth beautiful features and wearing an elegant emerald sari, Binita carried herself like a princess.

Dorothy demanded a tour of the new house. Mrs. Trinci was excited to show them around, her guests admiring the generous proportions and high ceilings of the rooms, the gleaming elegance of her brand-new bathroom, the considered lighting and windows, ensuring that her home had a welcoming cosiness through all the seasons.

"We haven't really started on the garden," Mrs. Trinci led her guests to the veranda. "My dear Sid had this beautiful new lawn rolled out a few weeks ago," she gestured.

"But it's the most magnificent tree!" Dorothy had heard all about the umbrella pine.

"Very special," agreed Binita. "And how unusual to find it right here!"

They stood in silence, admiring the great canopy which stretched over halfway up the lawn.

"I think we may have found a clue about that," Serena murmured.

Dorothy and Binita turned with inquiring expressions.

"I'll leave that to Mum to tell," she smiled. "It's her story."

Dorothy tilted her head towards Mrs. Trinci. "I'm intrigued?"

"First," Mrs. Trinci gestured to the nearby veranda furniture, "let's have tea."

Serena rolled out a trolley, laden with silverware and a Royal Doulton tea service borrowed from the main house. There was a convivial babble as she poured, and Mrs. Trinci's guests fussed over Rishi, while Sid explained the felicitous circumstances that had allowed this new home to be built so quickly.

I hopped onto the sofa between Sid and Serena, feeling that it was only a matter of time before I was served my own refreshment. Mrs. Trinci had baked an extravagant Sicilian apple cake, a pastry base containing granny smiths stewed with raisins, pine nuts and smothered in vanilla custard. After everyone had been served a portion along with a cup of tea, I was still waiting for my own treat to be served. Beside me, Serena was leaning back on the sofa. Before sipping from her cup, she instinctively dipped the tip of the ring finger of her left hand in the tea and flicked it in the four cardinal directions.

Opposite, Binita raised her eyebrows. "Are you Buddhist too?" she queried.

Serena nodded.

Dorothy turned to her fellow guest. "It's the Dalai Lama

Effect, my dear," she explained. "If you stay in McLeod Ganj long enough, we'll make a Buddhist of you too!"

Sid intervened quickly. "not that it's necessary to be a Buddhist. His Holiness would never say that."

Sid knew Binita better than any of them.

"That's true," confirmed Mrs. Trinci, shooting him a glance before turning to Binita. "He always says that his purpose is to promote happiness. So, you can be a happier atheist, or Catholic, or whatever you already are. You take what is useful."

Serena nodded.

"And this," Binita was looking at Serena again with a questioning, but not unkind expression. She gestured flicking, "You find it … useful?"

Serena was pensive for a moment. "That's a good question," she replied. "Truth is, I've been doing it so long it's become a habit. But, I hope," she shrugged modestly, "a useful one." She looked at Binita's inquiring expression. "You see, when I do it," she flicked, "I'm making a wish for all beings to also enjoy delicious food and drink. For them to have mundane and supreme happiness."

"It's about recollecting the wider reality," Sid leaned forward in his seat.

With unexpected and sudden clarity, I remembered how I'd eaten breakfast that day. No sooner had Tenzin presented me with food than I was eating it. Not for a moment had I considered the happiness of all living beings, wishing for them to also enjoy delicious food and drink. Much less had I 'recollected the wider reality'.

"There are many such practices," Mrs. Trinci responded to Binita's curiosity. "We consider the wellbeing of others as much as possible during each day."

Well, some more than others, I thought to my chagrin.

Eagerly devouring her food, Dorothy quipped, "You do this even when baking the most mouth-watering cake?"

"Especially then. If you spend a lot of time cooking, as I do, it is transformative. The Dalai Lama told me this personally."

It was Dorothy's turn to raise her eyebrows.

"Like today, when I was making this cake, I remembered all the beings who lost their lives so that we may eat."

"A cake?" Dorothy was taken aback.

"Of course," Mrs. Trinci nodded. "When land is cleared for crops, many animals lose their homes or are killed. They may be small, but they still have consciousness. Just like us, they only wish for happiness and to avoid suffering. And when farmers grow crops, they have to protect their livelihoods. They trap or poison mice and rabbits. They shoot deer and other animals – in Australia even wallabies. Fruit farmers kill birds."

Serena agreed. "That's before you even get onto pesticides and killing insects."

Sid was nodding. "We can't eat without others dying. Unless you live on your own organic farm, and you can control absolutely everything. Even food from a vegan store – how many insects are killed on the windshields of delivery vans?"

As Mrs. Trinci and her guests contemplated this, Binita looked taken aback. After a while she said, "I have never heard this point of view," she mused. "It makes sense."

Reminded of the starting point of the conversation, Serena looked back at her. "If we recollect others in this way, even if it's only for a moment, we are reminded of our relatively good fortune. Whatever problems we are having, when we compare our own lives …"

She didn't need to continue. It hadn't been so long since Binita and her daughters had been living in dire circumstances, after the death of her husband, Arhaan. The memory of it still vivid, she needed little prompting to recognize how dramatically her own fortune and those of her girls had changed.

"And so," wishing to brighten the mood, Mrs. Trinci gestured that the two younger women should eat. "We remember our very good fortune. Our karma to enjoy beautiful food. Our wish to become enlightened so that we can help others to freedom."

Understanding her mother's purpose, Serena smiled. She picked up a dainty spoon and was about to lift a glistening portion of cake to her mouth when I felt the need for a timely reminder. How patient is a cat supposed to be? Reaching out, I gave her a polite but firm prod.

She glanced down quickly. "Oh – HHC!"

"We are so busy wanting to help all living beings," lamented Mrs. Trinci opposite, "and forget our own Precious Treasure!"

"She'll live, Mamma," said Serena, responding to her mother's reaction – a trifle hard-heartedly I thought.

But Mrs. Trinci was already up and at the tea trolley, scooping a portion of custard and cream onto a saucer. It was only after she had placed it reverentially before me that Serena picked up her own plate again and began to eat.

I was about to lap at the delicious concoction with gusto, when I remembered Serena flicking her ring finger. The benevolent wish to be cultivated. How could I not? I heard and watched as the Dalai Lama invoked it frequently each day. I knew it by heart myself. The problem, always, was remembering to cultivate it!

The humans watched me indulgently, as they enjoyed their own food.

"You receive personal tuition from the Dalai Lama," Binita turned to Mrs. Trinci some minutes later, putting down her plate. "What an honor!"

"*Si, si.* I don't know why it happened to me."

"Perhaps this is not the first lifetime you have practiced *bodhichitta*," proposed Sid.

"*Bodhichitta*?" queried Binita.

"The wish to become enlightened for the sake of all living beings," said Serena.

Finishing my own portion, I lifted my head from the saucer and sat upright. About to lick my paw, in preparation for a quick face wash, I thought better of it. I was beginning to feel a little strange.

"This is the special ingredient the Dalai Lama told me to add to every meal," Mrs. Trinci confirmed. "I add it to everything. I think it improves the flavor."

Mrs. Trinci's assessment was altogether true. Startlingly accurate, as it turned out. So delectable was her offering that I found I had eaten it altogether too quickly. In the next moment

– it pains me to admit this dear reader, but I cannot pretend – I was unable to suppress a belch, the volume of which startled even me.

The humans looked momentarily surprised, before bursting into laughter.

"HHC!" scolded Serena, although she was smiling.

"Rinpoche!" exclaimed Dorothy.

Rishi giggled merrily.

After a few moments, when the hilarity had died down, I was back on track washing my face when Sid pointed out helpfully, "You know, a postprandial burp is thought to be a polite expression of appreciation in some cultures."

There were further chuckles. Less helpfully he continued, "Just not ours."

Redemption came soon enough. How could it fail to? Conversation inevitably turned to the subject of that afternoon's discovery and my own starring role. Serena went to the laundry, returning a short while later with the metal plaque, now clean and dry and revealed as an object of some antiquity.

For Dorothy and Binita's benefit, Serena recounted the story of how I had unearthed it. Mrs. Trinci read the engraving in her melodious Italian voice, "*Qui giacciono le spoglie mortali di Luna, la gatta prediletta di Padre Lorenzo. Requiescat in pace.*" Then translated, "Here lie the mortal remains of Luna, the favorite cat of Father Lorenzo. Rest in peace."

A sharp look suddenly came into Dorothy's eyes.

"What?" Mrs. Trinci wanted to know.

"Something's coming back about a Catholic priest

21

from Italy who lived in the mountains," she was glancing upwards. "Something from a long time ago. I'm afraid I can't remember …"

"Si?" Mrs. Trinci knew there was more to it than this.

"Well, it was, I don't know, I don't want to say," looking harried, Dorothy glanced around at the keen expressions now fixed on her.

"There was some … story?" prompted Serena.

"Definitely. A story," Dorothy looked relieved, "I don't want to say 'scandal', because I don't think it was quite that. Besides what used to be thought 'scandalous' eighty years ago …"

There were nodding heads.

"I can find out," she said.

Mrs. Trinci reached over and clasped her arm, beseechingly.

"Definitely," Dorothy nodded, glancing towards the tree. "After all, he was almost certainly the one who brought your beloved pine all the way from Italy."

"Who made it easy," Mrs. Trinci agreed, "for me to decide where I truly belong."

As everyone contemplated the most curious chain of events that had occurred, it was Binita who asked, "Do you believe this is karma? I mean, this strange coincidence?"

"As far as Buddhists are concerned," Sid explained, "nothing happens by chance. You could call it karma. But not as in fate, or kismet – you know, not something that was always going to happen."

"So," looking at Mrs. Trinci again Binita wanted to know, "You were the one who created the karma for it to happen?"

"Most karma comes from past lives," Mrs. Trinci told her. "We made the causes then to have what we experience now. But in this life, we create *conditions* for past karmas to germinate. Without conditions, karmic seeds can never come to life, whether good or bad."

Binita took this explanation in her stride. She was evidently heading, clear-eyed, towards a particular recognition and wanted it confirmed. "By doing this," she mimicked Serena flicking her ring finger, "and remembering *bodhichitta*, you are creating the causes for amazing things to happen?"

"My dear," Mrs. Trinci reached out, taking Binita's hand in her own, just as she had watched the Dalai Lama do a thousand times. "It is much better than that. When you take these practices to heart, little by little *you* begin to change. You see the world with a new mind. When that happens, you come to realize there is more magic in this world than you ever dreamed possible."

Chapter Two

Picture the scene, dear reader: rain-filled clouds are swirling down the mountains, plunging the afternoon into a state of foreboding gloom. Outside The Himalaya Book Café, thunder roars like a ferocious deity, discharging bolts of wrathful energy across the whole of Dharamshala. Inside is a benevolent sanctuary of warmly lit coziness. The restaurant is half-full of diners, happy to while away the time over a dessert or coffee until the tempest passes. The bookshop, up a few steps at the back, has half-a-dozen tourists perched on chairs or lolling on the sofa, engrossed in volumes they are reading in the restful glow of vintage lamps.

Usually, I would be sprawled on the top shelf of the magazine rack, enjoying a post-lunch siesta. But today I have been drawn to the most powerful source of light in the establishment. A warmth that comes not from one of the picture lamps hanging over the elaborate brocade thangkas, angled in such a way that the Buddhas themselves seem to emanate their lustrous colors. Nor from the alluring gleam of the brass-based lamps ranged along the windowsills, luring travelers to this place which is such a delightful convergence of cultures, East and West. No, the warmest of all glows is emanating from the living, breathing and frequently chuckling form of Yogi Tarchin.

Yogi Tarchin isn't a monk, but he is revered as a meditator, *siddha* and inspiring teacher. Rinpoche, as he is generally known – a Tibetan title meaning 'precious one' – has the warmest brown eyes and an ageless face, his grey moustache and goatee giving him the appearance of an archetypal Tibetan sage. More than anything, the first thing you notice about him is his radiant sense of lightness. Of joy. The indefinable but powerful sensation that even though you can see and touch him, his presence is somehow more subtly energetic than physical, as though he is barely there at all.

He had arrived with Serena soon after me, before the weather had suddenly turned threatening – it had been a glorious morning only an hour before. The two of them had sat down in one of the banquettes and it was only a few minutes before Franc, the owner of the establishment, had joined them. His French bulldog, Marcel, soon scuttled from his basket under the reception counter, to curl up at their feet.

In my own time I, too, responded to the magnetic attraction of the yogi. Having licked my saucer clean of that day's *plat du jour* with lip-smacking relish – a delightfully piquant *bouillabaisse* – I headed towards the banquette, hopping up next to Serena.

Heidi, the lissome young yoga teacher and co-manager of The Sukavati Spa, had arrived to meet her boyfriend, Ricardo, who was finishing his shift as the café barista. Responding to a wave from Serena, she approached the table. Bringing hands to her heart, she bowed to Yogi Tarchin in greeting, before sliding into the banquette next to Franc. "I was hoping I might see you somewhere," she glanced at Serena before looking in her purse. "I've been cleaning out the kitchen cupboards in our new place and found this. I brought it in for HHC." She placed a small tin on the table and fixed me with a blue-eyed smile.

"New place?" asked Serena.

"Ricardo and I are moving in together," her eyes sparkled, as she shot a glance in the direction of her handsome Colombian boyfriend, who was untying his apron.

"Congratulations!" Yogi Tarchin twinkled.

"I'm sure you'll be very happy" Serena smiled, reaching over for the small tin, inspecting its label before showing it to me. "Little Princess," she read the brand name. "Don't think you've had this kind before."

"Seemed a pity to waste it," shrugged Heidi. "Especially when I know a little princess who might enjoy it."

"Quite right," agreed Serena, replacing the tin on the white tablecloth, next to a brass stem vase containing a single red rose. "I can take it up to the monastery if you like?"

"*Danke schön.*"

It wasn't long before Ricardo slid in next to Heidi, nodding respectfully towards Yogi Tarchin. Early thirties, with glistening dark eyes and a stubble beard, he was the Latin yang to her Teutonic yin. The two of them huddled, all loved up, just as Sam came from the bookstore, where he'd left his assistant, Filomena, at the counter. Pale-faced and hair disheveled, far from his usual geeky acuity, Sam was looking foggy.

"Bad night?" Serena was sympathetic as he sank down next to me.

He nodded. He and Bronnie were new parents and four-month-old Piper was keeping them up all hours.

Across the table, Ricardo delivered a reassuring nod. "That double espresso will kick in," he smiled. "Ten minutes at the most, maybe five."

"Sure hope so," Sam smiled wanly.

It was snug around the banquette, with the cozy familiarity and warm banter of friends. While an elemental storm raged outside, in the most curious of ways it felt like we weren't gathered here completely by chance. As though some quirk of karma had happened to draw us together at this time.

And indeed, you too, dear reader. But why? For what purpose?

Serena explained how she had brought Yogi Tarchin into town to buy a few gifts ahead of his journey – tomorrow he was due to fly to Delhi, and then to Victoria Falls.

"My brother, Norbu, moved there many years ago. He keeps asking me to visit," Rinpoche explained. "I have decided the time has come."

"I'd love to go to Africa. All those animals!" Serena's eyes gleamed.

"Norbu works in a wildlife sanctuary," said Rinpoche. "He wants me to meet his elephants."

"I can imagine how *that* will go," responded Franc, beside him. "Elephants being so intuitive."

The others around the table were nodding. At the same time, however, I observed a shadow pass over Heidi's face.

"Very special beings," agreed Rinpoche, turning to Franc. "Norbu tells me it's true that they remember people and events many years later. He has seen it for himself."

Heidi's expression of disquiet was deepening, as though Rinpoche's words only confirmed some troubling thing. What was it about the conversation that upset her? The sentience of elephants seemed an unlikely cause for distress. Her unease was so great that Serena had caught her expression and was looking at her solicitously. Sam was studying her, puzzled. In time, Franc turned and, seeing how she looked, also became unsettled.

Suddenly, the whole restaurant was ablaze in phosphorescent white, followed moments later by a gigantic crash. My whiskers tingled.

After the rumbles had subsided, Heidi looked at Rinpoche, "What I find so ... hard about Buddhism, is this idea that animals have no souls." She shook her head. "Humans neither. In some ways, Buddhism is so close to my way of thinking about consciousness. But then there's this ... nothing idea about no spirit, no soul."

"Ah, *shunyata*!" Rinpoche nodded, at the same time

appearing light and untroubled. "It can be a difficult subject," he acknowledged.

On either side of him, Franc and Serena leaned back against their seats. Heidi, it appeared, had come up against a *Dharma* obstacle that was very familiar.

"It's true that in Buddhism we have no idea of a soul or spirit, like in other religious traditions. No permanent self or essence. This is not something we have."

"You see!" Heidi's face was crunched in an unfamiliar expression of anguish. "This is so sad."

"Is it?" Rinpoche shrugged, in an easygoing manner. "Why?"

It took her a while to find her answer. "What's the point of your life, what's the point of doing anything, if I turn into nothing when I die?" Before he could respond, she said, "Not nothing. I understand that. But no more Heidi."

"Correct," he agreed. "No more Heidi." Then after a moment, "You have a strong feeling of being Heidi, of Heidiness, that you don't want taken away?"

"Of course!"

"Good!" His eyes were lucent. "Remember this. Hold on to it tightly, because it is the idea to be refuted."

"Refuted?" Heidi exclaimed, as a new clap of thunder rolled across the sky.

"The idea we generally have of ourselves is quite unfortunate," Rinpoche had an inclusive way of speaking, as if he was like everyone else, rather than a highly realized yogi. "We have this notion of a being who is the size of a human with a mind the size of a brain. An idea that's fixed and very small. Limited. But in reality, no permanent thing can ever be found. Not about us, not about any phenomenon in existence. *Everything* is in a state of constant change."

"Everything?!"

He nodded.

"What, like …" she was glancing about the restaurant until her gaze settled on the table in front of her, and the tin she had brought in for me. "Like cat food?" she challenged, as though the idea was obviously crazy.

Yogi Tarchin followed her eyes, his shoulders beginning to quiver the way they always did when he chuckled. "Cat food?" he mused. "This is a *very* good example."

Franc and Serena exchanged a look of anticipation. It seemed that they had both heard Rinpoche extemporize on this subject before and were looking forward to a repeat performance.

For their part, Heidi and Ricardo were studying the yogi closely, trying to take in this new and extraordinary notion.

Head resting on the banquette, Sam was doing his best to stay awake.

"Is this the cat food you mean?" Rinpoche asked, gesturing towards the rose in the stem vase.

Confused by his deliberate doltishness, Heidi reached for the tin beside it. "This," she handed it to him.

For a moment, Yogi Tarchin studied the label. "Cat food is just a label, yes? Just a convention we all agree on. What's in this tin," he shook it in a way I would have found quite entrancing had I not recently had lunch. "Is not cat food from *its* side."

Heidi and Ricardo were puzzled.

"If Kusali were to take this to the kitchen and empty it into a bowl, the chef would probably say it was ..." he read the can. "Succulent tuna. He might even use it."

"Avocado Ritz!" laughed Serena.

"Not if I have anything to do with it," Franc was droll.

"It is part of a tuna, maybe the not-so-nice parts ..."

"Sorry HHC," interjected Serena.

" ... that have been put into a tin," continued Rinpoche. "And we label it, 'cat food'."

Heidi and Ricardo seemed underwhelmed by this observation.

"Two months ago, perhaps, this was part of a big beautiful fish, swimming in the ocean, when it was caught by fishermen. Did the tuna think it was cat food? Did the fisherman call out, 'Look at that shoal of cat food!'"

Focusing intently, Heidi shook her head.

"They are looking for tuna," confirmed Rinpoche. "Again, 'tuna' is just an agreed label for this kind of fish. So, they catch the tuna and part of it ends up in a tin. And one day it's put in a bowl for HHC – cat food, right?"

She was nodding.

"HHC eats it, and it's in her tummy. Is it still cat food?"

After a pause he continued, "What about the next day when she goes into the garden and ..." with his right hand, he imitated a cat's paw scratching a hole in the soil. "She goes to the toilet. What about that? Is it still cat food? Is it tuna, perhaps suitable for Avocado Ritz?"

About the table, faces were being pulled, before Ricardo ventured, "Cat poo?"

"Yes. Another label. We think it's disgusting. Horrible to look at. Putrid smell. But for the soil, very enriching. A few weeks go by and there is rain. The poo has disintegrated. It's part of the soil. The root of a bush is growing there and takes in the nutrients. Uses them to create," he pointed to the stem vase, "the most beautiful rose."

Around the table, his listeners turned as one to look at the graceful, cardinal-red petals of the bloom.

"Beautiful to look at. Perhaps the smell …?"

Serena lifted the bloom to her nostrils and inhaled. "Gorgeous!" she declared, before holding the vase for Rinpoche himself to enjoy.

Rinpoche glanced back at Heidi. "At this moment, a beautiful rose. But in its past life, you could say – cat poo. And before that – tuna. And before that, whatever tuna eat – small fish? Plankton?" He fixed her with a reassuring gaze. "Nothing comes from nothing. *Everything* is in constant change."

Heidi and Ricardo were nodding, following his explanation.

Rinpoche leaned towards them. "Same with us," he said. "The continuity of discontinuity, Chogyam Trungpa used to call it. This is why we don't talk about the essence of a person. Of some permanent being. Even within one human life – which is very short – the little girl Heidi aged six is different from Heidi aged twenty or fifty or the elderly Heidi at eighty. We use the same label our whole life, for something that's always changing. But in our mind, we believe it is more than just a label – we think there is something else there. Something we make up and believe to be true, because that's what everyone else is doing." He paused, looking over at Serena.

"Selfing," she nodded. "Concretizing something that's just an idea. Trying to make it seem permanent."

"The idea I have of myself," chimed Franc, "has gone through big changes throughout my life. I know it's been the same for you," he met Heidi's eyes.

"*Ja*," she glanced down.

There had been a time, sitting around this very table, when Heidi had shared her own grave self-doubts about her abilities as a yoga teacher. How her classes were so very different from the old-school approach of her Uncle Ludwig at The Downward Dog School of Yoga. Measuring herself by the yardstick she thought he applied, and threatened by the self-doubt she had battled as a teenager, Heidi had been in utter despair, believing herself to be a failure.

Pouring her heart out to a sympathetic audience, it had been Serena who had told her to ignore 'The Shitty Committee' in her head – in many people's heads – whose chorus of 'You can't' and 'You don't have what it takes' undermines all self-confidence. Franc, meanwhile, had counselled her on the importance of mindfulness. Becoming aware of negative thoughts about oneself arising in one's mind, and learning to let go of them.

Now she was the very successful head of all group classes at

The Sukavati Spa. She was in love with the romantic Ricardo and the two of them were making all kinds of plans for the future. As Franc observed, this was now a very different version of Heidi.

"I remember you once saying," she glanced at Franc, "how this 'I' we talk about is just a temporary idea. A story we make up about ourselves."

"A mere concept," Franc nodded.

Heidi leaned back in her seat for a while, absorbing all that had been said. "I didn't understand what you meant, back then. Not really. But what you're saying," she was looking back to Rinpoche, "is that 'Heidi' is just a label for something that is constantly changing?"

Rinpoche nodded once, slowly.

"We are the ones trying to make it feel permanent, concrete. And this is somehow unfortunate," she was looking back at Rinpoche. "But why?"

"Well, it doesn't accord with reality," he shrugged. "And if you were stuck with Heidi and Heidi-ness, the most you could ever hope to experience would be more of the same. Even in this lifetime, we are going through constant change. But to take a wider view, your consciousness, my consciousness, is something that has always existed. Unborn, because it was there before we, personally, came into being. Unceasing, because it continues in some way after we die. Not the same something," he held Heidi's gaze. "This is true. Instead, it is open and spacious like the sky. A continuity of awareness that has the potential to be a 'this' or a 'that', depending on what propensities are present.

"As human beings, we have the opportunity to take control of those propensities. To eliminate negativities. To cultivate the causes of wellbeing, so that our future experience of reality is not simply positive. It can be extraordinary! There is no reason we can't free ourselves completely from all limitations and abide in a state of ever-increasing bliss."

After a pause, Ricardo asked with a mischievous smile, "Like a rose instead of cat poo?"

There was laughter around the table. Rinpoche leaned forward, elbows on the table, "From our perspective, a rose is good and cat poo – not so much. But without the cat poo, or something like it, there is no rose. When we find things difficult, when we're in pain, if we feel our life is like cat poo ..."

There was chortling around the table.

Rinpoche continued, "It is a mistake to believe it will always be this way. Permanent. That we will always live such a life. Nothing is permanent. Especially not the contents of our mind. The most negative circumstances can give rise to the most transcendent of outcomes. This is what the lotus bloom symbolizes. Thinking that we are this way now and always wish to continue just the same," he looked back at Heidi, "is like a failure of our imagination. It's like we can't imagine being anything except cat poo when we could, in fact, become the most beautiful rose.

"In Sanskrit we have a word, a name, for the flow of consciousness that is our mind: *tathagatagarbha*. It means 'Buddha nature'. It is the pristine quality of mind that has the potential to be awakened to true freedom." His eyes sparkled, "A lightness of being that is beyond concept."

Was I the only one at the table to whom it seemed as if Rinpoche was describing himself and other advanced practitioners in the tradition, like the Dalai Lama? Explaining, perhaps, why there was always the feeling, when you were with such people, that they saw the transcendent possibilities of whoever they perceived, and were able to reflect it back to them, awakening the often unexpected recognition in whoever they spent time with that, beneath the surface, their *tathagatagarbha* nature was ever-present and perfect.

Across the table, Heidi smiled. "Thank you, Rinpoche. It makes me feel very happy not to have a permanent essence."

Yogi Tarchin, Serena and Franc all laughed.

"I'd rather have Buddha nature."

"Yes," Ricardo was looking serious too. "The possibility of awakening."

Fixing Rinpoche with an earnest gaze, she asked, "Do elephants also have Buddha nature?"

"Of course!" he said. "All beings with consciousness, with minds, have potential. This is why we respect all beings with minds, all *semchens*. They have the same Buddha nature that we do. Who knows, they may even realize it before us!"

At that moment, there was a shift in light in the café. Looking up from the table and out the windows, the storm had blown over and the sky was revealed as a pristine blue, without a hint of the menacing darkness that had filled it only a short while before.

"Sky-like mind," observed Franc.

"Yes," agreed Rinpoche. "Like this. The darkest clouds are only temporary."

Sam's bookstore assistant, the studious Filomena from Lisbon, approached the table. She had a customer query she needed help with. Excusing himself, Sam left the table. He was followed a short while later by Heidi and Riccardo, bowing in grateful thanks to Rinpoche and wishing him *bon voyage* for his visit to Africa.

I decided it was time that I should be on my way home too, while the sun was out. Getting up from where I was sitting, I touched Serena's arm with my nose and looked over at Yogi Tarchin, wondering for a moment whether he, himself, might be thought of as cat food by my larger and much wilder relations, and trusting that they would never have the chance to act on such an idea.

Hopping down from the banquette, I headed in the direction of the café doors. Sam, Filomena and a customer were standing at the reception counter. The visitor was a one of those dapper Europeans, who occasionally find themselves incongruously cast into the dusty streets of Dharamshala. Part of a European Union team of environmental specialists, in his taupe linen coat, chestnut pleated trousers and shiny umber brogues, he seemed to belong to a fashionable *piazza* café or the sumptuously furnished reception area of a Riviera hotel, rather than a ramshackle town like ours.

"For many years," he was enthusing, "I have been searching for this book." He clutched a small green volume, *The Myth of Trees.* "It seems I had to come all the way to Dharamshala to find it!"

"It *is* very thought-provoking," Sam told him. "Which is why I like to keep a few copies in the shop."

"Your whole bookstore," he gestured fulsomely, "would be an inspiration, even if it was transported to London or Paris or Rome!"

As I walked by, I was drawn by an aroma suggesting something very different from his suave appearance. Powerfully herbaceous but of a kind I couldn't place, floral yet with earthy tones suggesting a sunbaked landscape far distant from here. It seemed to be emanating from him.

"My only regret," the man lowered his voice, his cultivated accent was similarly beguiling but hard to identify, "is that I haven't been able to find a book on the history of Dharamshala in the first half of the last century."

Sam was silent as he considered this, his encyclopedic mind scrolling through the possibilities. Furrows appearing on his brow he said, "The Kangra earthquake of 1905 destroyed pretty well most things," he shrugged. "From what I gather, nothing much happened around here until the Indian government offered the Dalai Lama refuge in 1959."

I was similarly engaged, considering the encyclopedic possibilities of the customer as I paused, inhaling the smudges of the invisible, citrus-like fragrance, the fading pungency of musk.

Sensing my presence, he looked down.

"What a magnificent cat!" he exclaimed.

Sam and Filomena grinned.

"Siamese?"

Siamese, dear reader? Can you believe it! I had been called a great many things over the years, but – words fail me!

"Himalayan," Filomena corrected him.

Beaming, he was reaching down to stroke my neck.

"Just a label," Sam reprised our recent conversation. So, he hadn't dozed through it after all.

His words came as a timely reminder. Just a label – Siamese – attached to another label – me. Hardly a reason to take umbrage. I was, after all, a cat of many names. And did it matter whether I was called HHC, Rinpoche, The Most Beautiful Creature That Ever Lived or even, my least favorite, Mousie Tung? The names were labels – other people's ideas of me. Mere concepts. Just as I was a mere concept to myself. That thought sent a jolt of energy through me, so that I suddenly scampered away from the visitor and out the open restaurant doors, laughter following in my wake.

LATER THAT AFTERNOON, I WAS LYING ON THE SILL OF HIS Holiness's room when Tenzin and Oliver came in with a tea tray. This was one of my favorite times of the day. The three of them would appraise current events and plan future activities. After which, as they sipped Darjeeling, their conversations would range over all manner of subjects, while I lay watching the sun set over the courtyard of Namgyal Monastery and the more distant Kangra Valley.

Among this afternoon's themes, Oliver, the large jolly Englishman who was His Holiness's Translator, told the others of a story he had encountered in a book on Sufi mystics.

"A wise master is walking along a path, when he encounters a cow patty. Sitting on top of it is a fly. The master bends down to the fly and says, 'Today is your lucky day, Mr Fly! Come with me and I will take you to heaven.' The fly flicks and twitches his wings, considering the offer. After a moment he asks, 'Is there cow dung in heaven?' The master shakes his head. 'Then I will stay here,' he says."

Smiles appeared on the faces of the Dalai Lama and Tenzin.

"Very good," chuckled His Holiness. "We are all like this fly, yes?"

Oliver agreed. "Clinging to the sense of self, even when we're given the chance of transcendence."

"In our tradition," observed the Dalai Lama after a while, "we have a unique presentation of *shunyata*. But in other traditions, I think, there is also this idea of letting go of the ego. Of emptying ourselves, if we are to experience the divine."

As was so often the case when His Holiness communicated, he did so with more than mere words. It was a feeling, an energy that continued after his two Executive Assistants had left the room and he came to the window to pick me up and hold me to him. Embodying the wisdom of which he had spoken, together we looked through the open windows to the distant mountains, a gentle breeze carrying fragrances of pine and rhododendron, the invigorating scents of the forests.

Without my being fully aware it was even coming from

me, I began to purr, a deep-throated sound of gratitude arising as a spontaneous accompaniment to this state of bliss. One in which there was no Dalai Lama, nor any Dalai Lama's Cat. One in which mere labels were cast aside, and dualities transcended. Instead, there was only luminosity, free from all limitations, the all-pervading rapture of pure great love, as boundless as the universe itself.

Chapter Three

What does an enlightened person look like? If you were to bump into a *bodhisattva* in a shop or café, would you know it? Does the fact that such beings are so far evolved on their inner journey, confer on them a glowing aura perhaps, or some tenuous but unmistakable vibrational tug? Or would it be their hemp clothes and crystal nose stud that gave the game away?

Does a saint – of any kind – have a divine demeanor? Even while inhabiting a form that may perhaps be gnarled, jowly or liver-spotted, might there be something about their presence, their behavior, to indicate that this is, indeed, a being of great realization?

Do Buddhas always act the same consistent way, or are they permitted a certain quirkiness? Do they ever lose their temper, or at least appear to? In short, dear reader, do we have the faintest idea about the inner condition of the beings among whom we live?

These were the thoughts passing through my mind one particular morning, when I ventured downstairs to attend to the call of nature. Or they may have been. I can't honestly remember. I *was*, however, pausing to take in the general busy-ness of that time of the day. Intrigued by the spicy aromas wafting through the monastery gates, from where market stalls directly outside served momos to early-morning commuters. Absorbed by the whine of scooters and scurrying traffic on the road outside, accompanying the piping voices and laughter of uniformed children walking to school. Immersed in the succession of staff arriving at our building, those who managed His Holiness's office, men and women I had known my whole life and who had become my good friends. How wise and kind I knew some of them to be. Might there be, among the myriad of beings passing by, a few who, like the Dalai Lama, were *bodhisattvas* too?

There are some moments when the world has never seemed so fresh, nor its possibilities so tantalizing – even to a feline of senior years like me. And in that Golden World moment, having spent a marathon session on Oliver's desk the afternoon before, being combed and brushed to ensure that my coat was primped to perfection, I was drawn to one place more than any other. Impelled by an irresistible impulse.

Not far from the steps to the building, a garden bed segued through an untended patch of sandy soil until it met a paved pathway. It was here that I took myself, rolling shoulder first onto the grey dust until the entire length of my spine was resting on it. Then I began to writhe. Relishing the gritty dust in my coat. Wriggling from side to side, the better to grind as much earth as possible against my skin.

As chance would have it, Oliver arrived for work within a few moments. Whizzing in by bicycle, he came to a halt outside the building, dismounted, then attached a chain lock to a nearby railing. As he was straightening to walk inside, he caught sight of me, twisting and turning.

"HHC!" he cried in astonishment.

As he approached, I continued thrashing from side to side. Alright, I'll admit I was showing off now.

"What's the meaning of this?" he demanded.

Meaning? Why must there be a meaning? Couldn't a cat enjoy a dust bath without a philosophical interrogation?

"Such a nice long brush only yesterday. Now look at you!" He reached down to my exposed tummy.

I batted his hand away and after a last few vigorous contortions, leapt to my feet and scampered away.

"Little wretch!" he called after me. Not, I noticed, without a certain amusement.

I continued on with my back-to-nature adventures. Beside Namgyal Monastery was a small garden dominated by a lone cedar tree, beneath which was a park bench for the use of anyone who wished to climb the few steps from the sidewalk. It was bordered by flowerbeds full of prolific balsam, portulacas and agapanthus, enjoyed mostly by residents of the nursing home behind. They would gather on the veranda throughout the day, like theatregoers in their wheelchairs, to take in the verdant display. And I would regularly visit, my presence having such an uplifting effect that in their circle I went by my most elevated title – Therapy Cat.

Today it was neither the residents nor the flowers that drew me onwards, but rather what I hoped to find: one of the beds contained a clump of that herbage most sought after by felines – catnip. His Holiness's Driver, who tended the garden, had planted the grass especially for me. Sometimes its lure was so potent I could catch a whiff of it, even from my windowsill one floor up next door. Today was not one of those days, however; as I reached the garden, I detected not so much as a hint of my favorite stimulant. What's more, no sooner had I arrived I found I was not alone. Mrs. Trinci's dear friend, Dorothy Cartright, was sitting on the park bench. Beside her was Serena. The two of them were so deep in conversation, they didn't even notice my arrival.

"It's been months since I last saw Bett," Dorothy was looking towards the nursing home. "She's getting on, you know. In her nineties. Physically quite frail, but mentally still sharp as a tack. And a font of knowledge when it comes to local history."

Vivacious and lovely as always in a coral-red, sari-style dress, Serena was following Dorothy with rapt attention.

"Just as I hoped, she remembered some things about the priest who lived up in the mountains." Dorothy jutted her chin in the direction of Sid and Serena's home. "And when we spoke, I began recalling more of the story too. It was a strange tale. Actually, very sad. And of course, it all seemed so much further out of town than it does these days."

Serena nodded, eager to discover whatever she could about the man who had lived in the cottage on their property so many years ago. The one who had been the benefactor of the towering and entirely unexpected Italian stone pine, which had been a powerful source of homecoming for her mother, Mrs. Trinci.

"He was a very strong man – fiery."

"Passionate Italian," quipped Serena. "Like Mamma!"

"Sallow skin, dark beard and broad about the chest. A barrel of a man," continued Dorothy. "He came out as a missionary to convert the masses. But he hadn't been here long before he began to change. Broaden his views. He soon realized that there's more spirituality in India than most Europeans ever dream of. Vital, living traditions."

Serena was nodding.

"Father Lorenzo had been exposed to contemplative practices in Italy by the Benedictines. That may have been what opened things up for him when he came here."

"Meditation?" queried Serena.

Dorothy nodded, "Bett reminded me of something that went around the European community when he was alive. How he used to say that he came to India to discover the other half of his soul."

Serena raised her eyebrows. "That couldn't have pleased the Church?"

"He disrobed," said Dorothy.

"Ah. So that was what you remembered the other day," said Serena. "You didn't want to use the word 'scandal' …"

Having approached the two women without being acknowledged, I hopped on the bench next to Dorothy. I was unused to being ignored.

For a moment they both turned, offering greetings while stroking my neck.

"Actually," said Dorothy. "the disrobing was only the start."

Serena was engrossed.

"It was *after* he disrobed, Bett reminded me, that he moved out of town to the mountains. He had hardly any money, only enough for the smallest cottage. Just a couple of rooms. For a while he lived as a *sannyasin*, a renunciate, studying the philosophies of both East and West."

"With his cat, Luna?" prompted Serena, caressing my neck.

Dorothy nodded. "That may have been the most peaceful time for him," she said. "But I don't think it lasted very long. A few years, maybe. I remember hearing about the priest living in the mountain. It would have been around then. What Bett told me, and I didn't know this, was that he had a number of teachers. Gurus. One was an Indian woman named Uma."

"Splendor," Serena gave the meaning of the Sanskrit name.

"And she *was* very splendid, beautiful both inside and out by all accounts. Younger than Padre Lorenzo, but very evolved, coming from a family of rishis and maharishis. Anyway, the two of them became very close. Not so much teacher and student anymore, but more than that. In the end, they seemed to discover that they were true soulmates."

Serena smiled, nodding. Was she thinking, perhaps, about her own relationship with Sid, another unexpected and mystical union between East and West?

"They got married in a civil ceremony, and that was when the trouble really began."

Serena's face clouded.

Dorothy continued, "There was a dispute. A local family believed Uma had been promised to their son. Arranged marriage."

"Had she been?"

"Who knows?" shrugged Dorothy. "Seems there was a confrontation. An attempt to hurt or capture Uma by the man and his family who felt wronged."

"Heavens!"

"Lorenzo, being strong and rugged, stepped in. He quite literally threw his weight around."

"Good for him!"

Dorothy pulled a face. "Only it wasn't. Good for him, I mean. For either of them. Nobody knows what happened after that, except that it was only a short while later that someone set fire to their cottage one night, when they were asleep. Did a thorough job of it. The whole place was soon in flames. Uma woke and tried to save Lorenzo. But it seems that he'd already lost consciousness from the fumes. She was dragging him outside when she herself caught fire."

Serena's face twisted in distress.

"She made it," Dorothy confirmed. "He didn't. After that night, she was never seen again. She'd told someone, when all this unpleasantness was beginning, how they wanted to move far enough away that they might never be found." She

49

met Serena's sorrowful expression. "After the fire, that's what she did."

"And the people who caused it?"

Dorothy shook her head. "No one was ever charged. The family who had been making all the trouble about the arranged marriage vehemently denied having anything to do with it. And it did seem that Father Lorenzo had other enemies."

Serena looked puzzled.

"His manner," explained Dorothy. "Passionate. Volatile. He may have been a deeply spiritual person, but he rubbed some people up the wrong way. European and Indian."

"It's a curious thing that, isn't it? How people who devote their lives to altruism and benevolence sometimes incite such hatred. A lack of self-awareness on their part, perhaps? Or intolerance?"

"In Father Lorenzo's case, I don't think the local British community was ready for him. The views he held wouldn't raise an eyebrow today, but at the time …"

Serena was nodding.

"As for the Indian community, there were those who felt he'd violated their traditions."

"A nonconformist troublemaker," proposed Serena.

"Even though he was nothing of the kind." A faraway look came into Dorothy's eyes, before she glanced at Serena. "You know, I met him once."

"Oh!" Serena exclaimed. "And?"

"Something Bett said jogged my memory. He came to the house, probably to see Daddy. He was a lawyer you know, did property conveyancing and the like."

"Maybe to do with the cottage?" prompted Serena.

Dorothy nodded. "Could be."

"Did he say anything to you?"

"Nothing I can remember. I just recall the silhouette of a man who seemed large, with a very big beard, talking to Daddy on the doorstep. The feeling of Otherness about him."

Serena looked wistful.

"Bett remembers him. She says he once met her mother with the three children in tow and said how children were to be envied, because they understand the world not with their heads, but with their hearts."

"Hmm," Serena smiled.

"Bett's parents," Dorothy shuddered, "thought him most peculiar."

There was a long pause before Serena said, "The only silver lining I can see is that at least little Luna wasn't caught up in everything."

Both women returned their attentions to me.

"Yes, that would have been awful," agreed Dorothy, scratching my forehead for a while, before I hopped off the bench towards the flower beds.

As I went, I heard Dorothy's voice, "Bett did mention one other thing. There were rumors that Uma may have been pregnant when she left. But who knows," she sighed. "It really was all a lifetime ago."

That afternoon I was in my usual spot on the Dalai Lama's windowsill that overlooked the Namgyal courtyard. As I dozed,

I dreamed of the tall stone pine in Mrs. Trinci's garden, imagining a large bearded man meditating beneath it. Understood by his cat Luna, but not by other humans. A man who had made the journey from teacher to learner, from narrow to broad. A being who was more evolved, but less accepted, because he no longer fitted in.

As I was dozing, an Englishman, a Scotsman and an Irishman were shown into the room. And no, dear reader, I wasn't dreaming this, nor am I trying to recall a joke. An international conference on homelessness was being held in Dharamshala; His Holiness had officially opened it the day before. Tenzin, the Dalai Lama's other Executive Assistant, was ushering the British delegation of a homelessness charity into the room – one of several to be granted a personal audience.

Usually such a group would take their seats in a state of awe-struck deference, soaking in the presence of His Holiness, knowing they were experiencing a personal highlight to be forever cherished. Not so, this group. From the outset, there was an awkwardness about them. The Irishman, a giant of a man named Seamus, seemed the most nonchalant of the three, as he flopped into an armchair next to His Holiness. On the other side, George the Englishman, dapper in a dark jacket and closely cropped beard, seemed unusually apprehensive as took his seat. Opposite the Dalai Lama, sharing a sofa with Tenzin, was Scottish Bill. With a completely bald dome and spectacles flashing, he was perfectly well-behaved. At least, to begin with.

After a little small talk about the conference, His Holiness asked the three men about their activities at the charity. Tenzin, ever the consummate diplomat, seemed to fade completely into the background, so that it was as if he wasn't there. George explained that he was the fundraiser and CEO. Seamus ran operations. Bill was in charge of outreach. Responding to a request from George about advice he may wish to offer, the Dalai Lama began talking about the importance of motivation. The paradox of being wisely selfish: that when we focus our compassionate attention on others, we, ourselves, are the first to benefit.

It was advice he offered on a weekly basis. A message I'd heard so very many times before that I was long past the point of questioning it. Only today, Scottish Bill flashed a glance of some irritation across the coffee table, as His Holiness warmed to his theme. "That loving kindness stuff is all well and good when you have the luxury of a roof over your head," Scottish Bill couldn't help interjecting after a while, color rising so that his whole head seemed to glow pink. "But when you're living tough on the streets, it's a different story."

Despite the vehemence of his protestations, not once, during the time he had been sitting opposite, had Bill been able to look His Holiness directly in the eye.

English George squirmed, the source of his trepidation now apparent.

Seamus the Irishman tilted his head, signaling that he didn't agree wholly with his Caledonian colleague.

His Holiness didn't skip a beat. "Even so," he acknowledged

Bill's point with a nod. "I notice that sometimes people who have very little can be the most willing ..."

"Benevolence is an indulgence when you're broke!" Bill was not to be dissuaded. "At least, where I grew up. It's the same living rough today. You can't trust anyone. You have to keep your wits about you, even when you're asleep. It's brutal out there. This going soft," he was shaking his head, "it's just not realistic."

"I think His Holiness was talking about *our* intentions," said George, trying to steer the conversation back to calmer waters.

The Dalai Lama glanced at him nodding. Before turning to face Bill, "But those you help, also. There should be wisdom, of course, in dealing with others. But even for them, there must be a place for compassion ..."

"You're out of touch," Bill shook his head vigorously. And still steadfastly unable, or unwilling, to make eye contact. "The people we help, they're suspicious – and rightly so. It takes time to win their trust. Talking to them about kindness to others when they are shown none at all ..."

"Bill was on the streets for several years," interjected George, before his colleague could become even more incendiary. "In fact, he's become quite well-known in Britain."

From a folder on his knee, he removed a paperback book and showed it to His Holiness. The cover featured a photograph of a younger Bill – with a Scottish terrier.

The Dalai Lama chuckled as he looked at the photograph. "Your dog is very nice, yes?"

"Aye. Found him on the streets, my Dougal," Bill's voice modulated to a different tone. "Thieves stole him as a pup, to get money. When they couldn't sell him," his glasses flashed fiercely, "they left him for dead."

His Holiness turned, raising his left hand and pointing towards the windowsill. "This one too," he said.

Heads turned to look at where I was sprawled out resplendently. Whatever evidence might have remained from this morning's dust bath was certainly invisible from where they sat.

"A fine cat!" observed George.

The Dalai Lama pointed first to Bill, then himself. "This, perhaps, we have in common? We are both animal rescuers!"

If the revelation had any impact on Bill, he certainly wasn't showing it. His gaze was still averted.

"Tell me," asked His Holiness. "Did you protect your dog when he was small and weak?"

"I wouldn't let any lowlife hurt him!" growled Bill.

"You found him food?"

"He wasn't going to starve!"

"Even when you had no money?"

"There's always a way." The Scotsman slumped back in his chair.

The Dalai Lama regarded him solemnly. "A friend of mine spent many years as a prisoner of the Chinese. Harsh conditions. Solitary confinement – but not completely alone. Even though they gave him very little food, every day he kept some crumbs. There was a mouse that visited him in his cell, you see. He made friends with it. They were companions for several years."

Bill was nodding.

"Even in such harsh conditions, it was still possible to develop loving kindness. To think about the needs of others, not only oneself."

It was a pause before Bill responded. "I get that, with the mouse. And with Dougal," he was shaking his head. "Give me animals over people, anytime." There was passion in his tone. "You know, I didn't rescue Dougal. Dougal rescued me!"

"You see," His Holiness replied, as if Bill had just proven his point.

"But earlier, you were talking about people!" objected the Scotsman, spectacles flashing.

His Holiness raised his eyebrows. "Other beings. Not only humans."

"Where I come from," said Bill, "humans and non-humans are separate categories entirely."

For a long pause the Dalai Lama regarded him carefully, as the source of Bill's misunderstanding became increasingly apparent. Then a mischievous glint flickered across his face. "Well, *here*," he raised both palms in the air, somehow suggesting not so much a place as a state of mind. "They are one category. *Semchens,*" he beamed. "Tibetan for 'those who have a mind'. All of us wish only for happiness and to avoid suffering."

"Well," Bill was taken aback. "You won't find me arguing against that." Aggravation seemed to be draining away from his face. And was it possible that, just for an instant, his eyes had alighted on the Dalai Lama's – before darting hurriedly away?

"The great Lama Tsong Khapa," His Holiness raised his index finger and was wagging it at Bill. "Always recommended that we first practice loving kindness with those for whom we feel authentic love. Like Dougal. Only then, when we are very familiar with the practice, should we extend our benevolence to include others. This is what you have done, yes?"

Bill didn't reply, glancing down instead.

"Now you take care of other homeless people?"

When there was still no response, George confirmed, "There aren't many nights you'll find Bill at home watching TV. No, he's under the bridges or the flyovers or the alleyways, wherever people are destitute."

"Very good example of how to widen the scope of compassion from only one *semchen* to include many," said the Dalai Lama. "This is the path of the true *bodhisattva*."

"Wouldn't call it that," grumbled Bill. Adding after a pause, "But I do like the *semchen* idea."

It was only now that Seamus the Irishman, who had said nothing at all so far, pulled himself upright in his chair and turned to the Dalai Lama. "It might not seem this way, your Holiness, but you won't find a more tender-hearted man than Bill anywhere."

"Nonsense!" glowered Bill.

"At the office we call him Jellybean."

"Jellybean?" His Holiness was confused.

"You know, the candy?" George was about to explain.

The Dalai Lama nodded, "Yes. I know jellybeans."

"Well, you see," explained Seamus. "He's hard on the

outside but soft as mush on the inside."

Understanding the meaning of the nickname, the Dalai Lama clapped his hands together in delight.

"Tripe!" Bill countered.

"It's true, so it is!" protested Seamus.

"Better than the alternative," interjected His Holiness.

All four men looked towards him, inquiringly.

"Soft on the outside," explained the Dalai Lama after a moment, "but hard on the inside." His expression had turned serious as he contemplated this. "People giving the appearance of what they are not. This is very common," he was pensive. "Much better," he nodded approvingly towards Bill, "to be authentic."

At that moment, Scottish Bill seemed able to hold His Holiness's gaze for long enough to feel the particular effect that so many people experienced in his presence. For the pristine purity of his own heart and loving kindness, so deeply hidden, to be brought to the surface with such overwhelming force it was as if a switch had been flicked, and he found himself at the center of a sudden and unexpected radiance. Helpless to do anything but surrender to the blissful sensation surging within him, as his eyes continued to hold those of the Dalai Lama, they were revealed to be a clear and pristine blue – at this particular moment, glistening with emotion.

It wasn't long before a twinkle appeared on the face of His Holiness, as he spoke directly to the heart of his Scottish visitor. "The world, I think, needs more jellybean *bodhisattvas!*"

A SHORT WHILE LATER, THE BRITISH DELEGATES WERE SHOWN out. The Dalai Lama had to attend a meeting in the monastery. I opted for a visit to the Executive Assistants because it was approaching tea time – a ritual which, in that particular office, was an institution.

Oliver, the son of an Anglican vicar, could hardly be more English. Tenzin, meanwhile, an aficionado of cricket and the BBC World Service was Anglophile to the core. As a consequence, tea was more than just an afternoon drink for the two of them. A tray would arrive and be placed, with some ritual, on a side table against the wall. For a few minutes, the tea in the pot would be allowed to draw. Then one of the men would rise from his desk, add a dash of milk to two bone-china teacups, and pour tea through a strainer into each, before serving his colleague with both tea and whatever delicacy had been sent up from the kitchen. In today's case, two slices of Nutella crunch.

"We had an unusual group in today," Tenzin told Oliver, once they were both seated with their respective cups of tea – and I, on the filing cabinet, had been served a saucer of milk.

As Oliver munched happily, he described the British delegation, in particular Bill, the 'jellybean *bodhisattva*', who spent so many evenings in dark and inhospitable places taking care of people on the street, all this time forcefully denying that he was, in any way, compassionate.

Oliver's eyes sparkled behind his glasses. "There's a

particular kind of person like that you encounter," he said. "Who are not at all what they seem. They can come across as curmudgeonly. Irritable ..."

"Growl at people."

"Exactly. Meantime, they're much more generous and open-hearted than the rest of us."

Tenzin was nodding. "Like this one," he held aloft the Nutella slice he was about to eat.

Oliver wasn't following him.

"Mrs. Trinci," he explained. "When she first started working here, she was volcanic!"

Oliver chuckled. "Yes, I've seen that side of her!"

"She used to terrify people," Tenzin chuckled. "Especially some of the monks from the rural Himalayas who'd never met a European before. I once found a monk hiding in a cupboard downstairs, he was so scared of her."

"Really?"

"The kindest of hearts," he continued. "But some people just don't get her."

I was recollecting what Dorothy had said about Father Lorenzo. How he'd been passionate and volatile and had made a lot of adversaries. Enemies who may even have cost him his life. Meanwhile there had been other people who felt very differently about him, including the beautiful and highly realized Uma, who discovered in him her soulmate.

"Mmm," Oliver was agreeing. "To the people who know her, Mrs. Trinci is the warm, beating heart of any gathering. Lavish and maternal."

"Just like this man today, Bill" agreed Tenzin. "His colleague said he was the most tender-hearted man in the whole organization."

For a while, both men contemplated this great paradox.

"Compassionate people don't always look kind-hearted, but I suppose in some way we expect them to."

"They don't behave kind-heartedly all the time either," agreed Tenzin. "But we feel they should somehow float about consistently being all sweetness and light."

"Talking of being consistent, d'you know where I found this one when I arrived this morning?" Oliver gestured to where I was lapping the last of my milk. "Rolling in the dust downstairs."

"By the hedge?" queried Tenzin.

"Yes."

Tenzin was nodding. "I think I've seen her there before."

"Quite extraordinary," observed Oliver. "Usually, she's so clean and groomed and loves a good brush." He was shaking his head. "Then today it was like she couldn't get enough dust into her coat."

"It's instinct, I believe," Tenzin told him. "Something about absorbing bacteria. They cover themselves in dirt, then ingest the bugs when they lick themselves afterwards. It helps their digestive systems."

"I see," Oliver was looking up to where I lifted my head from the now-empty saucer. "But just so contradictory. I always think of the Dalai Lama's Cat as this supremely sleek feline, on show for visitors. Not some feral beast rolling in the dirt."

Evidently, I hadn't shaken off all of that morning's dust bath, because in the next moment there was a violent tickle in my nostril and I sneezed. A drop of milk which had remained on my nose flew into space. Both men laughed.

I failed to see what was so funny.

"Perhaps we are being reminded not to confuse our perceptions with reality," chuckled Tenzin.

Oliver's blue eyes sparkled behind his lenses, "Our reality may be filled with Buddhas and *bodhisattvas*, and we don't realize it."

"Exactly," smiled Tenzin. "We may be living in an ocean of transcendence, and it's only our limitations that make us see it as ordinary. But what happens when we remove those limitations?"

"Through the practice of the *Dharma*," confirmed Oliver. "We may, in time, even perceive a bodhi*cat*tva."

Tenzin smiled. "From *her* side," he mused, "no sleek feline. Nor feral beast in the dirt."

"Just so," Oliver looked up at me as I began washing my face. "What we see in the beings around us reflects our own subjective minds more than any objective reality, however it may seem."

Exactly, dear reader. And I have every confidence that your own projection of the Dalai Lama's Cat is utterly sublime!

CHAPTER FOUR

Do you carry an amulet, dear reader? A lucky charm offering you protection, no matter where you go or who you may encounter? I am not talking about a St. Christopher medallion, a Hamsa pendant or any other icon attached, perhaps, to a glittering chain around your neck. Not a physical object. No, the talisman I'm referring to is of the more powerful mental variety. A personal treasure you take with you everywhere. A jewel that, whenever recollected, is a source of true joy.

For my own part, I never thought much about amulets of the mind. It took me until I was a senior cat to discover their very existence. But they offer a unique form of protection. One that cannot be bought and is therefore priceless, in the truest sense of the word. One that can't be given by someone else to us, however kind their intentions. We must each choose our own personal talisman, because only we know what will work; once chosen, in time we may come to regard it as our most treasured possession.

Like so many great discoveries, mental amulets were something I encountered quite by chance. I had got into the habit of visiting The Sukavati Spa in the afternoons, after lunch at The Himalaya Book Café and before returning home. Simple curiosity had led me there to begin with – the grand old building, Sid's home before he married Serena, had been converted into a spa, offering aromatherapy, gong baths, yoga classes and all manner of other esoteric delights.

Sid and Serena's friend, Binita, managed the place with the cool assurance you might expect of someone who had once run a large family estate. Heidi, the svelte young German yoga teacher, organised group activities. From before dawn until well after sunset, the place was vibrant: students and customers coming and going, sprawled out on lawns or in one of the many reception areas, therapists working from their rooms, upstairs and down, and uniformed staff bustling with trays of freshly crushed juices and delicious cuisine. In other words, the perfect spot for a cat to be entertained by humans.

There was just one catch. Although the road from The Himalaya Book Café to The Sukhavati Spa was short, if somewhat uphill, a new family had moved into one of the houses en route, bringing with them a pair of snarling rottweilers, who would launch themselves from the shadows, baying ferociously at the top of their lungs, frightening the life out of me. The first time it happened, I scampered away as fast as my wobbly and somewhat elderly hind legs would allow. I was terrified that the beasts would somehow break free.

The second time, I was right outside the gates of the house before I remembered what had happened previously – and the same thing happened again. Only this time, I was somewhat less spooked. The dogs were secure behind the fence. They posed no threat. What I felt was not so much fear as rage. How dare the two slavering fiends treat me like this? I meant no harm. Unlike them, I was minding my own business.

After I'd hurried past, they launched into another barking frenzy – this time their focus was a silver-haired gent walking his equally senior dachshund on the other side of the road. Taken unawares, the two of them, like me, picked up their pace, hurrying away from the infernal din.

Long acquainted with this well-worn route, there was a third time that I unthinkingly headed up the road towards the spa. This time I remembered just before reaching the house. Once again, the two barbarous hellhounds broke loose, and there was nothing I could do except hurry past, my ears pressed firmly back in indignation, fuming at the commotion.

Since then, I had avoided the street. Outrage is an unpleasant emotion, is it not? In an instant, whatever good feeling we may have had is gone. All inner peace evaporates. Worse still, as I'd heard over many years of teachings from the lamas, anger is also very dangerous. A moment's anger, karmically speaking, may be all it takes to obliterate countless virtues. So great is the power of the unchecked mind, it can undo all the good we may have created over a very long time. Why undergo the extreme unpleasantness of the two dogs and court karmic disaster, when it could be avoided – albeit by taking a much lengthier route to The Sukhavati Spa?

Which is just what I did the next time I visited, taking a lengthy detour via a back alley behind The Himalaya Book Café and up a ragged road which ran parallel to the one where the dogs lived. It was a more tiring journey and by the time I reached the lush oasis of the spa, I needed a rest. The gardens and reception rooms, however, were full of people. Unwilling to be the center of attention – the curse, alas, of stardom in McLeod Ganj – I edged round the perimeter of the house to get away from the hubbub.

It just so happened that one of the ground floor windows of the private bedroom wing was open. Burglar bars offered protection from intruders, but were wide enough to allow the passage of a fluffy body. Within moments, I had hopped onto the sill, through the window and down into the room, behind curtains which were fully drawn. Emerging from behind them, it took me a few moments to adjust to the semidarkness, but I instantly recognized a scent.

Binita! I was evidently in her room, and she was lying on the bed oblivious to my arrival. I knew this, not from sight – the top of the mattress being too high above me – but from the barely audible sound of her breath. Just as I knew, from the special perception that we cats have, that she wasn't asleep. Just resting.

I hopped onto the bed, landing with somewhat less finesse than I would have preferred, given the condition of my unsteady hind legs. Startled, Binita flinched. But only for a moment. Quickly recognizing me, she reached out to pat the duvet next to her.

"My little friend," she whispered.

Making my way over, I touched her nose with mine, whiskers tracing her cheeks, before turning to settle where she had indicated. Soon I was sitting, paws tucked under me, staring into her eyes.

Binita was a woman of regal elegance. According to Sid, in her younger days, as one of the most beautiful women in India, she had been swept off her feet by a self-made man of great charisma and wealth. However, the wealth turned out to be more apparent than real. And when Arhaan died of a heart attack in his early forties, he had left his family millions of rupees in debt. Within weeks, Binita and her three girls had been living in poverty in New Delhi.

It was only her friendship with Sid, going all the way back to her teenage years, that saved her. On hearing what had happened to his friend, Sid had gone to the rescue. The Sukavati Spa had been his creation, turning his former home into a business that Binita could run. She had trained as a beautician and her daughters had followed in her footsteps. Furthermore, she had that indefinable bearing of someone of eminence and *savoir faire*. A person who, quite effortlessly, commanded respect. Managing a large property with many staff came easily to her.

I had heard all about the ups and downs of Binita's drama before she and her girls had arrived in McLeod Ganj. Just as

I'd witnessed the remodeling of Sid's creaking old house into a welcoming mountain sanctuary. And from the moment we had met, there had been a special connection between Binita and me. A feeling almost as if we'd known each other from an earlier time. I heard her once tell Serena that her sister, Yazhini, who lived in New Delhi, shared her life with Maya, a Himalayan cat strikingly similar to me. Which perhaps explained the otherwise unaccountable feeling I had when I was with her, that ours was a family connection. And why, as well, even though I had never visited her in her room before, it felt perfectly natural to be sharing her siesta.

But there was something unsettling at this moment. After reaching out to caress my face, Binita let her hand fall beside me and closed her eyes. For a few moments. Rolling on her back, she stared at the ceiling for the longest time. Then she was over on her side again, eyes clouded and expression drawn. She seemed to have come to her bed not to doze or sleep, but to withdraw. But why? What for? These were things I didn't fathom at first.

THERE WERE SUBSEQUENT AFTERNOON VISITS. ON THESE occasions, I headed away from the spa directly to the bedroom wing and through Binita's open window. Like most felines, I am nothing if not a creature of habit. And just like that first visit, it was to find the lady of the house lying on her bed, and far from restful.

I am embarrassed to confess that it wasn't until my third

visit that I came to recognize emotions that later seemed so obvious. I was entirely used to the Binita I observed outside, the elevating presence whose mere appearance brought out the best in those around her. The one who calmly managed an ongoing whirlwind of activity while warmly welcoming guests, dispatching constant orders and all the while preparing for what was to come. *That* Binita who was so assured, so capable, turned out to be only one dimension of the person I believed I knew. A part which I had mistaken for the whole. Because this other Binita, lying on her bed in a darkened room, was broken and despairing.

The difference was so stark it took me a while to believe my own senses. How could a person be one way outside a particular room, and yet so very different inside? It was troubling to discover her helplessness, to feel unhappiness seep almost palpably from her troubled form as we lay on her bed together.

One particular day, she had been sitting at a desk in one of the reception rooms of the spa, tapping on her laptop. For a few moments she looked away from the screen into the distance, and I saw a return of that heartbreaking anguish illuminated by the blue light of the screen. In a moment, I walked to her, rubbing her ankles with my body.

"HHC!" As she leaned to stroke me with her right hand, she brushed a tear from her eye with her left. "My little angel. Come to watch over me."

Flattering though that idea may have been, it wasn't true. As you know better than anyone, dear reader, I am neither angelic nor do I possess any protective powers. But it was troubling to see Binita this way. So I was relieved when I visited one afternoon, about a week later, to find her having a heart-to-heart with Serena in the garden. The flowerbeds of Sukhavati Spa had been laid out in a flowing natural fashion, creating trellised nooks and bowered grottos, some furnished with tables and chairs, others set with just a wooden bench, or a water feature gurgling among sandstone blocks.

It was in the latter place that I saw them, distant from the house. Three year old Rishi was playing on the lawn nearby. It was just the spot for a private conversation. In her emerald sari and hair tucked into an elegantly braided bun, Binita looked every inch a spa director. But as I approached, from her unguarded demeanor along with the intense expression in Serena's eyes, I suspected they weren't talking shop.

"It's not something you should be beating yourself up about," Serena was saying.

"I thought I'd put it all behind me," Binita shook her head. "Left it in Delhi where it belongs. I wanted to start a new chapter here. A clean slate."

"Of course." Serena glanced down. They were sitting on either side of a football-sized globe of stone from which water emerged at the top, glistening smoothly around its sides into a square stone trough beneath. The perfect place, as it happened, for a cat to quench her thirst on a hot day.

Serena was staring, unseeing, at the water, before she said, "You know, you're probably going through a grieving process, which is completely natural. I don't mean grieving for Arhaan, necessarily. I know you have very mixed feelings about him.

But your whole way of life. Everything that was normal for you and the girls. You know the seven stages of grieving?"

"I've heard of them."

"Denial's the first one – disbelief. That's followed by pain. Anger ..."

"There was plenty of anger in Delhi," Binita was nodding. "Especially when we were reduced to squalor. My fury about Arhaan's lying and cheating! It was like an energy that kept me going. I was determined he wasn't going to destroy us. Hema," she named her eldest daughter, now 25, "is still furious with him."

Serena looked pensive as she nodded.

"What comes after anger?" asked Binita.

Serena met her eyes. "Depression."

Binita rolled hers. "So, I'm a textbook case?" Her expression was wry. After a pause she said, "Before we came here, life was a daily battle for survival – there was no time to think. Then Sid and you came to the rescue and brought us to this wonderful place." As she glanced around, she caught sight of me and put her hand down to coax me towards her. I approached her, headbutting her leg, before sliding my body across her ankles and moving towards Serena to greet her too.

"You can't blame yourself for his deceit. You were a victim of it."

"I do blame myself," Binita was firm. "For all the times I suspected that things weren't right, but chose to do nothing about it. There were little clues – even not so little ones – right from the start. Instead of calling him out, I looked away. Like all his investors and creditors, I wanted to believe his lies, even as he was telling them."

"As young girls," countered Serena. "Especially in India, it is ingrained into us this idea of loyalty to our husbands."

"Loyalty," agreed Binita. "But not foolishness. I do blame myself for what I allowed to happen to the girls. I didn't only let myself down. I let them down too."

There was a long pause during which Heidi's voice carried across the lawn from where she was holding an outdoor yoga class, guiding her students through flowing vinyasas. Then Serena said, "Well, perhaps you did make mistakes," she held Binita's gaze. "Perhaps you were wrong to trust him. Not to call him out. But we're all human. We all have our frailties and failings. All we can do is learn our lesson and move on. Focusing only on the negative – what's to be gained?"

Binita adjusted her sari. "I expect you're right," she said. "Besides, most of the time I keep myself far too busy for introspection."

"I'm sure."

"I don't know if that's just avoidance?"

Serena flashed a droll smile. "A psychologist friend of mine often says that we don't think it's foolish for a deer to run away from a tiger. Sometimes avoidance is the right thing to do."

"Until the tiger outruns the deer."

"Yes," she nodded. "It may not be a permanent cure. Even if we outrun one situation, if we haven't fixed the underlying problem, it may only be a matter of time before the same thing, or something else like it, resurfaces."

I hopped up on the stone next to Serena. Her talk of running and avoidance had me instantly recalling the rottweilers. The outrage they provoked in me when hurling themselves at the fence in a frenzy of barking. The long detours I'd been taking to keep clear of them. Yes, I was by-passing them and the anger they triggered. If avoiding the cause of anger wasn't the best thing to do, what was?

"What would be a Buddhist treatment for my depression?" Binita asked now.

Serena met her gaze thoughtfully. "There are so many techniques," she said. "Different strokes for different folks. And I'm no expert at matching what's suitable for whom." She glanced away for a long while before saying, "The overall approach is often called 'opponent practices'."

Binita tilted her head in inquiry.

"The idea being that our minds, in their natural state, are completely clear. Whatever we put in front of them, they reflect. Allowing them to reflect only what appears to us in the outside world is a sure cause of unhappiness, because the nature of reality, of *samsara*, is a variety of different kinds of dissatisfaction. According to the *Abhidharmakosa*, this world is infected. Even when there are some really good things in our lives, there will always be causes of dissatisfaction, even profound pain." Serena shrugged her shoulders. "So, the way to deal with it is to take your mind elsewhere. Take this mind of clear knowing, which reflects whatever it is shown, and show it something uplifting."

"Mind training?" confirmed Binita.

"Exactly. In Tibetan, they have this word '*ga*' which means happiness – from contentment all the way up to pure bliss or joy. And '*mi*' means not. So '*mi ga*' is non-happiness. *Ga* and *mi ga* are like oil and water – they never mix. They don't coexist. You can't be joyful and angry in the same moment."

Binita was following her closely – as was I.

"Depression is a form of hatred. Instead of hating others for causing us pain, we hate ourselves. And the biggest danger of any negative thinking is the way it can easily become habitual. We get so used to thinking negatively that it starts to be our norm. Our whole view of reality becomes colored by it. Even if we're in a nice place, physically speaking, we're still angry or depressed."

I knew this to be true. On my journey here today, walking along a lush green verge, I had been seething about the dogs that had forced me to make my detour. And I knew from my previous visits to Binita that the bed on which she was resting, her room, the wing, this house, would be seen by many as a most extraordinary palace in which to live. Yet she had been deeply troubled.

Serena continued, "The way to counter our anger or depression, to stop it becoming habitual, is with an opponent practice. We find a mental antidote, something that really does give us joy, that genuinely lifts our heart and mind, and choose to focus on that."

"A mental antidote?" queried Binita.

"That's right."

"Like what, for example?"

"Something we know to be true that makes us feel happy.

Like: *I am always free to choose how I think* or *The best is yet to come.*"

Binita looked surprised. "Those don't sound at all like especially Buddhist thoughts," she said.

"They don't have to be. Opponent practice can be used by anyone. The main thing is to choose a personal antidote, a mental talisman if you like, that we personally find meaningful. And then recollect it throughout the day – *especially* when we're about to go into a situation where we may be challenged. We are deliberately putting a positive idea in front of our clear knowing mind, instead of a negative one. What we're doing is attracting the positive. The beneficial. The uplifting."

Binita was holding her gaze, nodding slowly as Serena explained this vital element of the claw of attraction.

"The more we do this, and the more acquainted with the positive thought, the more likely it is that the thought will arise spontaneously in the future, because one mind moment leads to another. More and more, the positive idea begins to color our experience of reality. We see the world through the lens of our attitudes, like wearing sunglasses. We're deliberately choosing a positive perspective instead of the opposite, which is getting sucked into a spiral of negative thinking, where one unhappy sequence sparks off another one, and before we know it, *everything* becomes a source of pain."

While Serena had been speaking, a curious faraway look passed across Binita's face, and a gleam came into her eyes. "I like the idea of a personal talisman," she said eventually. "And while listening to you, it was the strangest thing; I was reminded of a *sadhu* who used to visit us when I was growing up. I haven't thought about him for years," she was shaking her head. "But I did just then. I don't know if he ever gave the same advice. But I had this feeling, an intuition, almost as if he was tugging my arm right now and saying, 'Yes! Listen to her. *This* is what to do!'"

As she glanced down, Binita's eyes filled with tears. Serena reached over and squeezed her hand.

After a while Binita asked, "Do you have a personal talisman?"

Serena nodded. "Tibetan Buddhists are lucky. We have so many to choose from! We call them 'objects of virtue', a virtue being something that brings you happiness. Our main one is *bodhichitta*: 'For the sake of all living beings I attain enlightenment'. Or we might have 'How lucky am I to enjoy this life of leisure and fortune!' Or 'As I think, so I become.' Or 'My guru is kinder to me than all the Buddhas.'"

Binita raised her eyebrows.

"Combined with meditations on these subjects, the more we invoke them, the more they shift our thinking."

Once again, as Serena was speaking, she seemed to evoke a parallel wisdom for Binita.

"There was an idea like this the sadhu taught," she began smiling. "I can't remember exactly – it was such a long time ago. Something about 'In this city of Brahman there is a lotus shrine', meaning that in my body," she raised her fingertips to her heart, "there is a place I can go to find peace."

For the longest time, she held Serena's gaze before bringing her hands together. "Thank you, Serena, for your wisdom."

"Oh, not *my* wisdom," Serena quickly corrected her. "But I'm very happy to be passing it on."

"And thank you, HHC, for your visits. You know," she glanced from me to Serena, "this little one has come to me several times when I've been feeling down. She senses something, I feel."

Serena reached out to stroke me. "I'm sure you're right," she said. "Rinpoche is the most perceptive little creature."

THAT AFTERNOON I TOOK THE DIRECT ROUTE HOME PAST THE dogs. As usual, they were tormenting every passer-by, their special ferocity reserved for anyone on a bicycle or walking a dog. I knew that their violent displays were nothing but warm-up performances for when I walked by. But I was determined to do so without getting angry. I had my own new personal talisman, after all. An amulet I hadn't had to search for, since it had arisen in my mind the moment that Serena had started giving examples to Binita. *How fortunate I am to be the Dalai Lama's Cat!* I knew it to be true. It was a thought that always gave me joy. And not just in a cerebral sense. I *felt* it with every sinew of my somewhat portly, wonky and ageing form.

Choosing to focus determinedly on this uplifting notion, as I continued past hell's gates, wasn't something that would otherwise have occurred to me. But I did so now. The rottweilers came out, baying frenziedly. But there were no ears pressed back from me on this occasion. I didn't scamper, nor did I even quicken my pace. If anything, I dropped back to the pace of a leisurely stroll, while contemplating my immense good fortune. Glancing in, I noticed that the two beasts were straining on their leashes. It seemed they were tethered to ropes that didn't – quite – allow them as far as the fence or gates. In reality, no one was at risk of being attacked. It was all bark and no bite.

By the time I'd made my way past the property and the barking began to recede, my view of the beasts had shifted. They were rabid and ferocious to be sure, but there was something pitiable about them. And on future encounters, eager to try out the power of my anger-subduing amulet once again, as I walked by the gates, because I was less susceptible to their frenzy, I noticed more about them. The dull coats. The lean frames. In truth, the two of them were desperate creatures.

The next time I visited Binita in her room, she wasn't lying in the darkness but sitting on her bed, reading a volume with an elaborately designed cover: *The Upanishads*. Along with her perfume, I was instantly aware of a scent of sandalwood. I soon detected its source. On her dressing table, in front of a vivid image of the elephant god Ganesh, was a stick of incense with a glowing tip.

"I found it, HHC!" She patted the bed next to her and I hopped up. "That verse the sadhu used to repeat."

Putting the book down, she closed her eyes. Evidently, she was learning to memorize it. "*There is this city of Brahman and in it there is a small shrine in the form of a lotus, and within can be found a small space,*" she quoted. "*This little space within the heart is as great as this vast universe. The heavens and earth are there, and the sun and the moon and the stars; fire and lightning and wind are there, and all that now is and is not yet – all that is contained within it."*

Finishing, she turned to me, eyes gleaming. "It's beautiful, is it not?"

I stepped over nuzzling her hand with my face. She soon began stroking me.

"The sun and the moon and the stars. All that now is and is not yet. This is who we are, not so? Who we *really* are. Not just a person sitting on a bed. *This is* my talisman."

I began purring.

"I think it always was. Somehow, I lost it. Then Serena brought it back to me. How lucky are we, HHC?"

What Serena had told us was true. Our minds are like glass and will reflect whatever we place before them. Focus on darkness and discord and what can possibly arise other than misery? Broaden one's perspective to what is uplifting and wholesome, and the result is equally predictable.

How fortunate I am to be the Dalai Lama's Cat!

It was also true that the more you deliberately recollect a thought, the more likely it is to pop into your mind for no reason at all at different times of the day. Sprawled out on the top shelf of the magazine rack at The Himalaya Book Café, I might be gently dozing off the effects of that day's *plat du jour*, when I recollect my mental amulet – and feel an abiding glow of warmth inside.

Serena had said that when a talisman is *combined with meditation* on a subject, it gains a special power. With a belly full of food in a cozy environment, it was easy to reflect on my good fortune. But when it came to my own mental treasure, its power was derived from much more than the great variety of treats and indulgences bestowed on me because I was His Holiness's Cat. More than the visiting celebrities and spiritual teachers to our home, who were a source of ongoing intrigue. No, the most important reason I felt so fortunate to be the Dalai Lama's Cat was because of what I experienced through him. The knowledge that reality is, more than anything, mind's creation.

It was a truth made tangible in his most fleeting encounters. One clearly apparent to individuals, even when among an audience of many thousands of people. And when it was just him and me, meditating each morning together, how extraordinary! To spend hours in the presence of one whose panoramic mind abides effortlessly in a state of infinite altruism, what other possibility can there be than to experience limitless bliss?

How fortunate I am to be the Dalai Lama's Cat!

That's *my* mental amulet, dear reader. What's yours?

Chapter Five

Wʜᴀᴛ ꜰᴏʀᴄᴇ ɪꜱ ɪᴛ ᴛʜᴀᴛ ᴘʀᴏᴘᴇʟꜱ ᴜꜱ ᴏɴ ᴏᴜʀ ꜱᴘɪʀɪᴛᴜᴀʟ ᴊᴏᴜʀ-ney? Why is it that, one day, we may sense the most extraordinary rapture and insight doing the selfsame thing that, for weeks, months or even years, has produced no special feeling in us at all? Is there something we can do to have such an experience more often? To accelerate its onset? If so, what precisely is the special energy, the rare spark that sets us alight with sensations of transcendent bliss?

As the Dalai Lama's Cat, you might expect me to be privy to conversations about this subject, might you not? And you would be right. More to the point, however, is that I have had exactly such experiences myself. At apparently random moments. Including just last week.

His Holiness rises at 4 am every day to meditate for four hours – a practice he has maintained since he was a young monk in Lhasa. I accompany him during these sessions, which can sometimes feel very long indeed, notwithstanding several catnaps along the way.

On other occasions, like that morning last week, time itself seems to dissolve into irrelevance, as if it were only some trifling, made-up notion all along. There is, instead, a feeling of something that goes quite beyond words.

How to describe it? Perhaps with a metaphor.

Have you ever marveled at a spray of tiny, but brilliant rainbows cast by a suncatcher on a wall or carpet? Have you ever tried to seize one – pouncing on the dazzling but ephemeral jewel, as it swirls and shimmers from side to side? Or imagined how extraordinarily delightful it would be to succeed – to clutch a rainbow in your paws? Not only that, dear reader, but to ingest it. To swallow this most beguiling of trophies. To have the rainbow light permeate your entire form, radiating positive emotions, powerful and kaleidoscopic, so that your whole being is suffused in a blissful luminosity, seeming to belong to a different dimension. But most emphatically here and now.

That is what it feels like at such moments. At least, to me. The boundless joy is of a different order from any everyday gladness I might feel, having nothing to do with earthly things. It is quite beyond that. But at the time that it's happening, there is no sense of any other way of being. You perceive the whole of the universe, from the broadest sweep of space above you down to the very vibrating atoms of the walls around you, as divine.

That morning, the exalted sensation began to fade, like a rainbow dissolving back into who knows where. In the afterglow that lingered, I knew that I'd had an experience of the greatest of wonders. For just a moment, some unseen curtain had been lifted and I'd caught a glimpse of the ultimate truth about myself and everything around me. And as I tilted my head to face the Dalai Lama, he was looking directly at me and smiling.

He had ended his session but had yet to rise from his cushion. Getting up, I circled round him in an anticlockwise direction, tail held high. And as I brushed him with it, without any conscious thought on my part, it vibrated like a current was passing through it. An involuntary surge of gratitude for what I had just felt.

As I came round to the front, standing before him, our eyes met again. I had no doubt whatever that he knew exactly what I had experienced. No less, probably, than he did whenever he sat down. Bending towards me, he cupped my head in both hands and kissed me on the crown. Then in an oft-repeated dedication, he said:

"May the precious, superior mind of enlightenment,
Be developed in those who have not developed it,
And not decrease in those who have developed it,
But increase continuously."

These were lines I heard His Holiness recite frequently. But that morning, they seemed to hold a special significance. And an uplifting sense of the extraordinary stayed with me throughout the day. Whether observing the world from the windowsill as the Dalai Lama worked at his desk, or slipping outside to the courtyard that evening, as I took in sights and sounds with which I was long familiar, they seemed somehow different. There was a delightfulness to them, and it felt like even the most mundane of activities were part of a wider and numinous unfolding, in which everything was just exactly as it should be.

I WAS LOUNGING ON THE TEMPLE STEPS AS DUSK FELL, ENJOY-ing the balmy afterglow as the sky ripened by degrees from dusty orange through to deep cerise, before all color drained away, leaving only a vast canvas of pale blue in which the first glittering jewels of the night began to sparkle. Over at the monastery, warm orange squares appeared along the sides of the buildings. An evening breeze gusting up from town brought the aromas of a thousand evening meals. From near me came the sounds of sandalled monks, mopping and drying the temple entrance and steps and heaving open the two great entrance doors, with their elaborate brass handles and displays of eight auspicious objects. It wasn't long before the first attendees appeared for that evening's class.

The temple was used most evenings by the Namgyal monks, but on Tuesdays an open class was offered by Geshe Wangpo, which anyone could attend. My first inkling that this was a Tuesday night was when a group of regulars from The Downward Dog School of Yoga appeared. Ludwig, the founder of the yoga school, straight backed and silver maned, accompanied by Merrilee carrying a tote bag, Ewing Klipspringer in his trademark tennis shoes, and Suki, petite and fluid, with her mop of dark curly hair.

Geshe Wangpo was one of the most revered lamas at Namgyal – a Geshe Lharampa, meaning that he had attained the highest of all scholastic levels. He was also one of the most well-loved. His Tuesday night classes were not only popular with the monks at Namgyal, who were soon streaming in, leaving their sandals strewn on both sides of the temple doors. The townspeople also loved his classes for the clarity of his teaching and his preference for interaction over monologue. Franc, owner of The Himalaya Book Café, was coming up the steps now, accompanied by Ricardo and his girlfriend Heidi. Sid, Serena and Mrs. Trinci happened to come through the gates of Namgyal at the same time as Sam, the bookstore manager. The four of them were chatting as they headed inside, pausing to greet me with a tickle on the neck, Mrs. Trinci once again reaffirming that I was The Most Beautiful Creature That Ever Lived.

Sometimes I went to class too, but I hadn't decided about this evening. At least, not until I caught a distinctive whiff of something. It was enchantingly exotic, but I'd smelt it before. And not long ago. It suggested a rugged, sun-drenched and foreign vista, verdant with orchards and flowers. Rising to my feet, nostrils flaring, I turned to discover the bearer of this fragrant benefaction was the linen-jacketed European I had encountered a few days before at the book café. A few steps behind Sam, Sid and Serena, he too reached down to offer an affectionate stroke.

Sam was taking off his shoes. As he did, he noticed the man behind him.

"Oh!" he smiled. "You came!"

"I had a quiet night to myself," replied the man with a faint trace of an accent. "So, I thought why not?"

"Your colleagues?"

"Gone home." He was untying the laces of his brogues.

"Uh-huh."

"Extra week to myself."

Sam was about to follow the other three into the temple.

"Sit with us, if you like," he pointed inside.

The other man nodded. As he bent towards his shoe, he glanced towards me. And from the moment our eyes met, I felt connected to a person who was not only a lover of cats, but one who combined a penetrating intelligence with the sensibilities of an artist. Someone who had spent much time exploring arcane passageways and esoteric chambers – whether in real life or metaphorically, I couldn't say. However, despite the regular appearance of this forty-something European with the sandy hair and hazel eyes, I had no doubt at all that he was a man of many secrets.

In an instant, I knew I must attend class. Following him into the temple, we walked down the center aisle until we got to the row, about halfway towards the front, where Sam and the others were taking their places on burgundy meditation cushions, bedecked with embroidered golden lotus emblems. Soon after, I was sitting with the visitor to my left and Sam to my right.

There was a vibrant silence among the rows of students. Serena, Sid and Mrs. Trinci were ranged to the right of Sam in this sanctuary of wonder and peace. Flickering butter lamps lit up the golden faces of Buddha statues at the front of the room. Incense drifted evocatively from the altar. The atmosphere, redolent with expectation, was so still that you could hear the soft clunk of the dowels at the bottom of the *thangkas*, blowing against the walls in the evening breeze.

Geshe Wangpo arrived, with that round, muscular physiognomy of Tibetans, emanating a *prana* as bracing as it was heart-melting. He prostrated three times in front of the Buddhas before settling on the teaching throne. Following the prayers and mantra recitation that always came at the start of class, the lama opened his eyes and looked at his students, taking his time to slowly scan the room, as though surveying who was here and how best to connect with them.

"Each one of us wishes to attain enlightenment," he began. "Or at the very least, to make progress towards that goal." His voice was deep and mellow, without being loud. As always, from his very first words, his audience became utterly absorbed by what he was saying.

"We have a great many practices to follow. As you know, we are not a 'one size fits all' tradition. Depending on your disposition, whether you like to engage with the world or spend time in solitary retreat, if you like reading and learning or doing practical things – then, no problem. We have many methods. All of them help cultivate the quality that propels us towards our goal of enlightenment. The quality ..." he paused to add emphasis to his next words, "of virtue.

"In Buddhism, we start with the view that reality is a projection of our mind. *Samsara* and *nirvana* are not so much physical places, as states of mind. Even in our everyday experience, two people can be standing in the same room, one filled with suffering, the other experiencing a state of profound wellbeing. Those different states aren't coming from the room and what's happening in it, or they'd both feel the same way. *Mind* determines wellbeing.

"If our ultimate goal is to experience the great bliss of enlightenment, we need to cultivate its cause. Which is a mind of great virtue."

Geshe-la briefly explained the law of karma, of cause and effect. How cultivating non-virtuous thoughts, views, habits, speech or actions could only result in suffering. And the opposite – how all enjoyment and feelings of wellbeing were the effects of previously created positive karma.

"This is simple. Buddhism 101," he smiled. "I'm sure we all understand. What I want to talk about this evening is the difference between good karma and the virtue that propels us towards enlightenment. You can be the kindest person in the world," he sat forward, his voice deepening with significance. "Forever giving your time, effort and material offerings to others, but not create the causes for enlightenment. Can anyone say why that is?"

It was only a few moments before one of the monks at the front raised his arm.

"Without *bodhichitta*," he responded, once Geshe-la nodded towards him, "there is no intention to become enlightened for the benefit of others."

"True," said Geshe-la. "This is the importance of motivation. And *bodhichitta* is the ultimate manifestation of loving kindness. There is none higher."

I remembered the recent tea party at Mrs. Trinci's new cottage. How she had told everyone about the Dalai Lama's advice to recollect *bodhichitta* every time she baked a cake, made a meal, or undertook just about any activity. How she had taken his advice so much to heart that remembering *bodhichitta* had become habitual to her. *For the sake of others, may this be a cause to attain enlightenment.* This was now recurring so often among her thoughts, it had become part of who she was.

"Along with *bodhichitta* should be the recollection of something in particular?" Geshe Wangpo was seeking another answer.

This time it was Sid just a few seats away who raised his arm, at the same time saying, "*shunyata*".

"Yes, exactly," Geshe Wangpo met his eyes. "Recollecting *shunyata* is essential. Also something we practice recollecting throughout the day until, ideally, it is a constant recognition."

Next to me, the European visitor had placed a handsome leather compendium on his right knee. He was turning its parchment pages over to an empty one, at the same time as retrieving a glistening cobalt-blue pen from his jacket pocket. Inspired by Geshe-la's words, he had soon removed the gold-trimmed lid, and his hand was moving quickly across the page, leaving lines of black script of a sweepingly elegant kind I had never seen before.

"When doing something kind, for example, when we remember there is no inherently existent me, doing some inherently existent nice thing for some inherently existent other person, *then* we create a cause for enlightenment." For a long while, Geshe-la remained silent, giving everyone in the temple time to process this information.

"What is enlightenment, after all?" he continued. "It is a word that means 'awakening'. Awakening from what? From the hallucination that what we perceive exists separately from our own minds. Which is why the actions we undertake while recollecting *shunyata,* what we might call awakened actions, are the causes for us to experience an awakened state. When we don't recollect *shunyata,* our positive actions will still have positive outcomes, but those outcomes will ripen within *samsara.* They lead to worldly enjoyments, such as wealth, long life and all manner of pleasures – but still experienced with the misperception of inherent existence, which is itself a cause of suffering."

A different occasion came to mind. That stormy afternoon at The Himalaya Book Café, when Yogi Tarchin had explained *shunyata* to Heidi, as it related to cat food. How 'cat food' was just a label for something which had no essence and was constantly changing. Just like us. How, no matter how hard you tried, you could never find a single atom of anything that was permanent, independent or existed from its own side.

"In the *Dharma,* we say that we need two wings to fly to

enlightenment," the lama flicked the index and middle fingers of his left hand up and down. "*Bodhichitta* and wisdom. We need the motivation, the intention for awakening," he nodded in the direction of the monk who had answered his earlier question. "And also, the understanding about how things exist, which counters our usual ignorance," his eyes met Sid's. "*Shunyata.*"

The visitor had continued writing, quickly filling a whole page of his compendium with words that were not only consistently shaped, but also adorned with beautiful curls and flourishes. As he wrote, a small gold star at the end of a scarlet ribbon marker, which emerged from between the cream pages, had been wiggling and swaying only inches from where I sat. It had taken every ounce of equanimity I possessed, dear reader, not to react. But as soon as our guest took breath, straightening from his labors and looking towards the teaching throne, I had my chance. Standing, I placed my left leg on his right thigh for leverage and leaned towards the compendium, batting the star at the end of the ribbon before catching it easily in my right paw, bringing it to my nose and sniffing it curiously.

If the man was surprised, he didn't show it. But he did glance down – as I sensed did Sam, and beyond him, the others. After a few moments, I became aware of even Geshe Wangpo's attention from the teaching throne. Lifting my head, I raised my face to this visitor from Europe with the elegant handwriting and the intriguing green eyes. Before I settled down beside him.

A question was being asked.

"You sometimes hear it said," it was Ewing the yoga student with the faint hint of a Californian accent, "that you can never do anything positive without benefiting from it personally. That even when you're, let's say, generous, there's something selfish about your actions, because you're just trying to feel good about *me*, and how kind and noble *I* am."

Geshe Wangpo was nodding as he listened.

"But recollecting *shunyata* is the opponent of that, isn't it? Because there's no donor, no recipient, no donation from its own side."

"Quite so!" The lama was approving. "*Shunyata* opposes egotism. Self-righteousness. Any feeling of superiority we might have. If we understand there is no self to be found, we aren't doing it for *me*."

There was a pause before a voice sounded. "But we kind of are, aren't we?" came a distinctively throaty voice. It was Merrilee from the yoga studio. A zany nonconformist with a big heart and rebellious impulses, she never shied away from expressing a different opinion. "Our future me," she said. "The me that benefits as a result of the good deed."

"This is a conventional view," Geshe Wangpo shot right back. "A view that clings to the idea of a separate self. But it is a view we want to free ourselves from because, at an ultimate level, it is inaccurate – *and* the cause of our greatest pain." His tone was gentle, but firm.

Merrilee seemed unconvinced.

"This future me," he challenged, "where is it to be found?"

She shrugged. "It doesn't exist right now, obviously. It's

just an idea."

"Just an idea," he pushed her. "Like the present me."

She pulled a droll face before saying, "If nothing exists the way it seems, and everything is just an idea, why bother doing anything?" She sounded vexed by the futility of it all. "We may just as well take happiness where we find it and live for the day. *Carpe diem*."

There was a ripple of skittish laughter about the room after her observation.

"Very good." It was as if Geshe-la had coaxed Merrilee into voicing something that most students would have never dared to. Were there others, perhaps, who shared her frustrations?

As in previous classes, we had returned to a recurring theme with Merrilee. Was the discipline of formal mind training necessary? Couldn't you simply live in the present moment, as much as possible simply being? Must you, all the time, recollect the wish to become enlightened for the benefit of others? When it came to awakening, why didn't simply abiding in the sublime gift of the present moment cut it?

"All of us in this room," Geshe Wangpo's expression was one of patient indulgence, "have a very good experience of *samsara*. We are human beings with leisure and fortune. We suffer, of course, but it's manageable. Some of us, perhaps, enjoy contentment and happiness a lot of the time."

Once again, the visitor was making swift flowing notes across the pages of his book. The ribbon marker, I noticed, was no longer dangling tantalizingly in front of me.

"But this experience of *samsara*," continued Geshe-la, "will definitely finish. In this life, we may lose the great love of our life. Or a dear child. We may suffer from a terminal illness. Even if we have a full and long life, it must come to an end. And if we haven't abandoned our innate sense of a 'me' or 'I', our own cherishment of self will propel us into a future rebirth. Maybe a good one, if positive karmas ripen. Maybe not so good. Even if it's very, very good, we will find ourselves, once again, where we are now. With a mind that is sometimes up, sometimes down."

Merrilee glanced down, acknowledging the roller coaster of her own emotional life.

Geshe-la shrugged. "It seems a bit pointless, continuing like this, life after life, if here and now, we could escape. But escape means a shift in perspective. Letting go of deeply ingrained habits of thought. And that requires application and effort. Just like physical training, it is hard work, especially to begin with.

"But if we practice virtue, this is a counter to our *samsara*. When our actions are motivated by *bodhichitta* and we recollect *shunyata*," he was flickering the fingers of his left hand again, "we create the direct causes for enlightenment. Not just regular good karma for happy conditions. Enlightenment karma – like a separate bank account. As human beings who understand the *Dharma*, we can create such causes constantly during each day."

Such was the sense of nearness, the feeling that what was happening was not so much a formal teaching as a conversation, that the visitor, without even looking up from his page, began to speak. "Why do so few people know this?" he said incredulously and – as was apparent from his own startled expression – to his own surprise. He glanced up at Geshe Wangpo somewhat apologetically.

Quite used to such responses, Geshe-la replied smoothly, "Because they don't have the karma to know it. Buddha himself said that to have a human life like ours, with the time and inclination to study the *Dharma*, is as unlikely as a blind crippled turtle, that comes from the depths of the ocean every hundred years, just happening to stick its neck through a golden yoke that's floating on the surface."

Our visitor was transcribing this fresh insight. I remembered how the Dalai Lama had told India's Top Ten Social Media Influencers Under 30 how, if they really wanted their lives to become meaningful, they could start to practice *bodhichitta* and *shunyata*.

A hand was going up two rows in front of us.

"Yes," gestured Geshe Wangpo.

"Creating positive causes without recollecting *shunyata*," an Indian woman was speaking. "Is this what I've heard called 'dirty good karma'?"

The lama smiled wryly. "I have heard this too," he said. "But even dirty good karma is much better than bad karma! Still, if the same action enables us to create the cause for enlightenment," he nodded significantly, "why miss the chance?"

She brought her palms to her heart.

"Being virtuous, in Buddhism, seems different from what we know in the West." It was another tourist, this time British by the sound of him. "Where I come from, virtue has strong moralistic connotations. People pay lip service to it, but in reality, many people see it as a bit old-fashioned, an ideal almost too much to live up to. But would you say that virtue is at the heart of spiritual practice?"

"Of course," Geshe Wangpo nodded. "No virtue, no transformation."

"And with virtue," he continued. "Can we expect signs of progress?"

"What signs do you mean?" the lama asked.

The tourist paused, "I suppose, peak experiences. Some kind of rapture. Joy of a completely different quality from usual."

Whiskers tingling, I was returned immediately to that morning's meditation session. How time had dissolved and bliss had surged within me, and the sensation was as though I'd been transformed by some inner suncatcher beaming dynamic, all-encompassing rays of love. I knew exactly that the visitor meant.

"These things you call … signs," Geshe Wangpo nodded. "They are very nice to have. Gifts," he shrugged with a smile. "They may happen from time to time. But they are not necessarily a mark of spiritual progress."

Then responding to the man's confused expression, "People also have such experiences from taking drugs, yes?"

The visitor shifted on his cushion.

"If we chase after unusual visions, intense feelings of ecstasy. If we seek otherworldly experiences, phenomena that can't be explained. This is like spiritual tourism, yes? Looking for a buzz. Something that will put us on a high. Until the memory fades and we need to find a new high. The next big thing." He paused, allowing his words to settle. "The real signs of progress," he leaned forward, his features softening, "are when we sense a lightness, an inner peace, no matter our circumstances, because the source of our contentment isn't coming from out there. It's coming from within. And when we find ourselves beginning to care more for others, whoever those others may be. Elderly people. Children. Animals who are struggling. When our compassion arises – this is another important sign of development."

Geshe Wangpo's own equanimity and benevolence pervaded the gentle stillness of the temple for a while, as his students – monks, locals and tourists – absorbed what he had taught them. Like so many *Dharma* teachings, this evening's class had combined ideas that presented a radically different view of reality, while at the same time being somehow self-evident. The basis of a life worth living.

Then Geshe-la was bringing the palms of his hands together for the dedication verses, with which he always concluded class: the *Four Immeasurables*, which were always chanted at the end, invocations of love, compassion, joy and equanimity:

> *May all beings have happiness and the true*
> *causes of happiness.*
> *May all beings be free from suffering and*
> *the true causes of suffering.*
> *May all beings never be parted from the*
> *happiness that is beyond suffering –*

great nirvana liberation.
May all beings abide in peace and equa-
nimity, their minds free from attachment,
hatred and free from ignorance.

AFTER GESHE-LA LEFT THE ROOM, AS WAS THE CUSTOM, THE locals and visitors remained in place, giving the monks and local nuns precedence to leave the room. Closing, with some ceremony, the compendium in which he'd been writing, ensuring that the red ribbon marker with its twirling star was neatly tucked near the spine of the book, the visitor removed the cap from the end of his sleek blue pen. As he did, he glanced over to where Sam was clicking back his ballpoint. He turned to face Sam and their eyes met. "I really must thank you so much for suggesting I come here tonight."

"My pleasure," said Sam.

"The words of your Geshe," the visitor gestured towards the teaching throne. "I have attended several Buddhist teachings before. But these …" the depth of his admiration was revealed in his eyes as he shook his head, "they were of a different order, completely. Good karma versus enlightenment karma. I have never heard this explained before. In a way it seems so clear."

"We *are* very fortunate to have him as our teacher," agreed Sam.

"And *I* am very fortunate to have met you," said the man, sincerely.

He was replacing the cap on his pen when Sam nodded

towards it, "By the way, that's a wonderful pen!"

Smiling, the man handed it to Sam to look at more closely. He was engrossed by the textured aquamarine sheen of the glistening barrel. The ornately patterned nib. The glistening cap with its decorative gold inlay.

"Magnificent!" he said, turning the pen over in his hands.

"Then, I'd like you to have it," said the visitor.

"What?" Sam, both perplexed and delighted, was immediately handing the pen back to the visitor. "It's too much!" he said. "It's an expensive pen – you can see that."

But the man's smile only grew broader as he refused to take it back. "If it helps you accept it, I work for the company that makes these writing instruments. I can easily replace it when I get home."

"Really?" Sam's eyes were gleaming.

"I insist."

Sam turned to Serena, who was sitting on the other side of him. "Look what I've just been given," he beamed, holding the pen aloft.

"Impressive!" Serena was admiring as, further along the row, was Sid, before she looked appreciatively towards the visitor. "We noticed someone else checking things out during class," she chuckled, glancing down at me. "It seems that your taste is much admired in McLeod Ganj!"

He met her eyes, laughing as he reached down to stroke my neck. "Yes, she was very curious. But alas, I won't be leaving my notebook for her."

"You're really quite certain about this?" Sam asked him,

rolling the pen in his hands.

"Yes."

"You can be sure I will always treasure it." Sam was thrilled.

"As will I treasure the advice you gave me."

"Inviting you to class?" Sam was staring at the gift.

"In the shop, earlier. When I told you of all the frustration I've been having with the local government, trying to access their archives. You told me to 'let go'."

"Oh, yes!" Sam glanced at him, nodding. "I remember."

"I stayed on, after the team went home, because I wanted to see if I could find out more about my grandfather, who lived somewhere near here. It was all a very long time ago. I've been battling every step of the way with the bureaucrats. I've done all I could in the past few days to get permission. When you said, 'If you really let go, sometimes doors open unexpectedly', it chimed with me," he nodded. "So, I did. No more archive request forms. No more writing letters or making inquiries. I've even given away my pen!" he grinned.

Sam nodded, encouragingly.

"I will spend my last few days here just soaking it all in. Admiring the mountains and the trees and all that my grandfather would have loved."

Getting up to leave, along with most of the locals, Serena, Sid and Mrs. Trinci waved their goodbyes. I stood up between the two men.

Which was when Sam exclaimed, "I've just seen it!"

The visitor nodded knowingly. He had evidently been waiting for the discovery.

Sam was noticing the cap of the pen, surprised to find that its gold clip was shaped in the elegant form of a seated cat, tail held high.

"I know that you're a lover of cats," the visitor was tickling under my chin. "So I thought this an appropriate gift."

"I do love her," agreed Sam. "Although she's not *my* cat."

"She was in the shop," the visitor was puzzled. "And here."

"Spends a lot of time with us," nodded Sam. "Mrs. Trinci," he motioned to where she had been sitting, "is her biggest fan. Tell me," he nodded towards the pen cap. "Where did the design come from?"

"Inspired by my maternal grandmother," the visitor replied. "And named after a cat."

Sam was nodding.

"And if I may ask …" prompted the visitor. "If this is not your cat, where does she come from? She's quite magnificent!"

"This," Sam looked at me indulgently, "is the Dalai Lama's Cat."

"Really?" It was the visitor's turn to be delighted.

"She lives with him here at Namgyal Monastery. Just across the courtyard."

"Extraordinary!" The visitor's hazel eyes were bright with astonishment as he met my own. "This has been, all round, the most intriguing evening," he said.

Sam was tucking the special pen in his jacket pocket with care. As the two of them prepared to stand, he asked the visitor, "You said the pen is named after a particular cat?"

"Yes," he nodded. "One who was most treasured by both

my grandparents when they lived here long ago. We call it the Luna edition."

Chapter Six

There are some beings who make their presence felt the moment they step into a room, are there not, dear reader? On account of their eye-widening good looks perhaps, or mesmerizing authority, or whisker-tingling serenity, there are those among us who have a certain sway, a charisma, that draws us to them.

Such a person was occupying a table at The Himalaya Book Café during one of my afternoon visits. I became aware of him before I even saw him. As I strolled through the swing doors towards my usual spot, pausing briefly to touch damp noses with Marcel, curled in his basket under the reception desk, I became aware of a deep undercurrent of laughter erupting from one of the banquettes. A sound that seemed drawn like rich warm lava from the subterranean depths, burbling and coalescing until it rose to such an unstoppable force that detonation became inevitable.

On the few occasions that we had disruptive diners, other patrons would soon be frowning in censure. Head Waiter Kusali, the supreme diplomat, would swoop to the offending table to deploy his unique combination of sternness and emollience. In short order, the aberrant visitor would fall into line. Or, on one occasion I had witnessed, be seen off the premises.

Today's unruly guest, however, had the opposite effect. Climbing to my usual place on the top shelf of the magazine rack, I soon identified the source of the laughter. A large round bald man in a yellow and green check shirt was sitting opposite Marianne Ponter, manager of the nearby nursing home. Always a neatly dressed professional, the very last person who would want to cause a scene, Marianne not only showed no sign of discomfort, she seemed quite in thrall to her lunchtime companion.

As did others around him. Fellow diners evidently found his laughter infectious. There were many chuckles and twinkling faces. He was a man who invited positive attention. He would respond to glances towards him directly, meeting others' eyes with a quip here or a rejoinder there, so that he was soon the center of a whirl of good humor. His laughter was by no means constant but had the effect of dissolving invisible barriers and the usual reserve. Fellow diners on their way out were stopping at his table for a brief exchange. The wait staff were drawn towards his table with an apparently magnetic pull. Even Head Waiter Kusali, hovering on the fringes, seemed strangely disarmed and indulgent in his presence.

Just who this visitor was, and what he was doing here, became more apparent when Franc, owner of the establishment, inevitably found his way to the table. As Marianne gestured towards him, her companion was on his feet, shaking Franc amiably by the hand. "Blake Ballantyne," his voice carried across the lunchtime buzz from the nearby banquette. Along with a sentence which included the words 'director' and 'Bohemians'.

At this point, dear reader, a quiver of fascination passed through me.

On the other side of the road from the small garden next to Namgyal, the one overlooked by the nursing home with the flowerbeds and catnip, a steep driveway led to the grounds of what had once been a sanatorium early in the last century. It had been decommissioned after the Second World War, and at various stages had been used as a hostel, an admin center and a storage facility, before being boarded up and not used for anything at all. It was a building with a certain presence, its elevation overlooking much of McLeod Ganj, while at the same time enjoying an uninterrupted view of the Himalayas behind it – towering waves of ice-capped ranges as far as the eye could see.

In all the time I'd lived here, I had only ever visited the old sanatorium once, when Heidi had taken an open-air class on its lawn one evening. It was a place of little interest to a cat, especially a senior one like me who needed a strong reason to climb up any vertiginous slope. In recent months, however, I had noticed builders' trucks and tradespeople's vans turning into the driveway in unprecedented numbers. From the bench beneath the cedar tree, I had observed the arrival of construction materials and those who knew how to use them. I had guessed that Christopher's dream was coming true.

A former resident of Marianne Ponter's nursing home, my dear friend Christopher Ackland had been an artist who, in material terms at least, had lived in both poverty and obscurity throughout his life. Rediscovered as one of the creative trailblazers of his generation soon after his death, the assortment of canvases left behind in the nursing home garage had been dramatically revalued. With help from Sid, Marianne had sold his paintings through a London gallery, and directed the millions of dollars they fetched to the cause Christopher had once whimsically suggested he would support if he ever came into money: a Sanctuary for Broke Old Bohemians. Which is to say, people like himself.

I had overheard Serena and Mrs. Trinci talking about how the old sanatorium was being remodeled. More recently, how the foundation overseeing the work was recruiting someone to run the enterprise. Now, it seemed, that person had appeared in our midst and one broke old bohemian's windfall was about to be used to support others, in a way he would never have thought possible.

Marianne Ponter was excusing herself to return to her desk at the nursing home. Franc was now sitting at Blake Ballantyne's banquette, the two of them deep in conversation. They apparently had good friends in common in San Francisco. Then, in a vortex of conviviality, Blake Ballantyne was on the move, up the few steps to the bookstore, where he began perusing the shelves, not far from where I was sitting. Sam gave him time alone, before approaching to ask if he could help.

"Are you the manager?" the visitor demanded, fixing an intense expression on Sam as he gestured the shop with an expansive sweep.

Sam nodded, somewhat nervously.

"In all my travels," Blake Ballantyne regarded him closely. "I have never encountered such a brilliantly curated collection of books."

"Thank you!" Sam was relieved.

"Blake Ballantyne," the other extended his hand.

"Sam Goldberg."

"Only a most evolved person could have brought together such an inspired list," Blake was still shaking his hand, while holding Sam's eyes. His accent was British, but with a softly Californian inflection.

"You're very kind."

"The very best of the Tibetan lamas, which one might expect to find in a Dharamshala bookstore," Blake had turned so that they were surveying the shelves together. "But the Western explorers too. You've got them all here – Blavatsky, Humphreys, Gurdjieff, Ouspensky. Paul Brunton. Bede Griffiths. The Christian mystics – Meister Eckhart, Saint Thomas, Saint Teresa of Avila. The Californian crew – Huxley, Isherwood, Heard. And, of course, the Beats."

From the way he spoke, Blake seemed familiar with the authors, and not simply from their books.

"Sounds like you know some of them personally," observed Sam.

"As a boy, I meditated among the loquat trees of Santa Monica with Gerald Heard and Christopher Isherwood."

"Amazing!"

"My Pappa was good friends with Allen Ginsberg. A fortunate upbringing." A low rumble started somewhere within his ample form. "I know I may seem old to you," the burbling grew in volume. "But Saint Teresa was even a bit before my time."

It was a subdued chortle compared with the more volcanic explosions from earlier in the café. His laughter filled the bookstore nonetheless, along with Sam's, and a gleeful connection was made.

Blake asked Sam about where he came from in California, and the two of them soon established that their mutually favorite store in Los Angeles was Book Soup in West Hollywood. Sam wanted to know more about the famous spiritual teachers he had known. Blake required little prompting to describe his encounters with Krishnamurti, who he declared to be one of the most elegantly dressed men he had ever met, with his tailored suits and Italian sports cars and living palatially in Ojai, California.

"He always made the same points, in his teachings," said Blake. "I know I can share these with you, because you'd understand," he flourished his hand in the direction of the philosophy section. "Why do you bother with questions like is there a God, or life after death, or some way to reach *nirvana*? Why do you identify yourself with some ego, some self, that can't be found? Don't you realize that there is no feeler, but only feelings, no thinker, but only thoughts? Wake up to the only thing there is – this moment, here and now. Focus on the eternal present. Don't get caught up in creeds which only strengthen the ego, by teaching that there is an 'I' to save or to become enlightened."

In just a few sentences, it was evident that Blake Ballantyne hadn't simply met a variety of gurus, he had also integrated their teachings.

Sam was following him, riveted. "This is something I keep returning to," he nodded, indicating what Blake had just been saying. "This idea we have in Buddhism that the self is an illusion. And at the same time, all these elaborate practices to free ourselves from that illusion. But do the practices themselves, in some way, reinforce the idea of myself as someone wishing to become free of a self?" For a while his eyes were fixed to Blake's, before he glanced away. "Sorry," he said. "I didn't mean to treat you like a therapist."

Blake was nodding thoughtfully. "It's a valid question," he replied. "And as it happens, I *am* a therapist. What you're talking about isn't only a concern for Buddhists, it has parallels across all traditions. In Christianity, the Augustinians believe that salvation isn't something that can be earned, but the Pelagians never doubted that for salvation to happen, your words must be backed up by your deeds. Do you choose a therapist to work on yourself, or one to help you accept yourself the way you are? All of us encounter this same tension on our inner journey."

Sam was staring at him, as though a hundred other questions were forming in his mind. But the assistant manager, Filomena, was coming over, asking for his help with a phone inquiry. Blake made his own request for a book, before lumbering back to his banquette, pausing to make light banter with another table of diners on the way.

It was fascinating to observe a man who seemed to connect so effortlessly with others. A larger-than-life being, so completely open to those around him that when his booming laughter sounded without restraint, he filled the room with an infectious lightness of being. At the same time, his was no shallow presence. His conversation with Sam had revealed a level of insight that made him all the more intriguing.

Binita appeared at the café entrance, strikingly elegant as always in a turquoise sari. Surveying the tables very quickly, she began making her way in the direction of where he was sitting, reading his tablet. I followed her closely. She was introducing herself, and he gestured for her to sit opposite. This was the time of the afternoon when I might have set out to visit her at The Sukavati Spa. It seemed that Binita had not only saved me the trip, but she had also made it easy to study McLeod Ganj's newest resident at close quarters.

I gave them a while to settle, a large pot of tea and two cups placed before them. Hopping from the magazine rack, as I padded towards the banquette where they were seated, I heard them talking about how future residents of the sanctuary might be granted discounted group rates for The Sukavati Spa. How spa therapists might visit the sanctuary to deliver their yoga classes, sound baths and aromatherapy to residents with mobility issues.

Blake was looking through a folder of documents about Sukavati that Binita had given him, when he caught sight of me approaching.

"Every good bookstore needs a resident cat!" he declared approvingly.

I jumped on the seat next to Binita.

"And what a beautiful creature!"

"She is," agreed Binita, drawing her fingertips together and massaging my forehead in just the right spot. "But you know, although she comes here and to Sukavati quite often, her real home is nearer you." She gestured up the street.

"Namgyal Monastery?" he queried.

She nodded. "This is the Dalai Lama's Cat."

"Ye Gods!" he boomed. "And every bit as magnificent as you would hope such a cat to be." Elated, he stretched across the table to stroke my neck. Glancing at him, in the instant that my eyes met his, I knew I was in the presence of that most special class of *homo sapiens* – the Cat Lover.

As Blake Ballantyne watched me settle, glowing with pleasure, Binita broadened their conversation. "If you don't mind my asking, I am sure that you had a very comfortable life back in California. Why did you decide to take this job setting up the sanctuary here?"

Across the table, Blake nodded. "It was a very congenial life in many ways," he agreed. "Beautiful facility in Carmel. Extraordinary visiting teachers. It was much more than a retirement estate. It was a place where people kept on growing right to the end of their lives, just as I hope they will here. The curious thing is that many of us over there had always sensed a kind of umbilical cord to India. A connection of an important kind."

His eyes on hers, it was as though he was looking into the liquid gaze and graceful features of a real-life Indian goddess. He continued, "Some had lived here. Some, like me, who had visited over the years, felt more philosophically connected to India than anywhere. So, when the opportunity came up to do pretty much what I was doing already, but in India, I seized it. For so much of my life I have yearned to experience living here, to immerse myself in the spirituality of the place. It was now or never."

"When you say 'spirituality', do you mean Buddhism in particular?" asked Binita.

Blake shook his head. "Also the Hindu tradition from which Buddhism flowed – the Buddha stood on the shoulders of giants."

She was nodding.

"I am intrigued by just about all religions, as long as their devotees don't try to convert me," he chuckled. "The intriguing smorgasbord of beliefs and practices in the subcontinent is extraordinary," his gesture was expansive. "*Dharma*, whatever its source, is something that moves us closer to enlightenment. The rich bounty of *Dharma* insights here is a source of fascination for many of us in the West."

Binita smiled wryly. "So funny," she was shaking her

head. "The first thing most Indians aspire to do, as soon as they become rich, is to move to London or America. My late husband was one. He really thought he had made it when he bought a home in Regents Park."

"Yes," Blake shared the irony. "Constantly yearning for what we don't have. And the West has so much to offer materially."

"But not, for you, spiritually?"

While always cordial, Binita was usually reserved when it came to discussing matters like personal beliefs with people she didn't know. It seemed that she, like Marianne Ponter, who had been sitting where she was only a short while before, also felt at ease with the large, loud but beguiling man sitting opposite.

"I was born and brought up in Surrey, and all I knew was the Church of England. It was only much later that I came to learn about the true breadth and depth of Jesus's teachings. How only a tiny fraction made it into what is generally known as Christianity today. The version I grew up with had a distinctly imperial flavor. Growing up, I always assumed that God must be British."

Such was Blake's theatrical delivery, that Binita couldn't help laughing.

"It's true!" he boomed, his laughter resonating.

"Heraldic flags draped all the way down the cathedral. The monarch as head of church. Next stop, heaven. Everything ordered and in place. The dreamy spires and stained-glass windows, the Kings College choir that sang like angels. For me, I found great beauty in it all, but no depth. Where was the divine connection, spoken of by the likes of Saint Thomas and Saint Teresa? How to attain it? The church seemed fixated on statements of belief and its own rather outdated moral code, but curiously uninterested in what *I* regard as our real purpose, which is connecting to the divine within."

Raising his right hand, he was touching his heart. "It's astonishing how through all the centuries, so little time was generally spent on letting go of the verbalized rituals – the hymns, however soaring and the prayers, however elegant – simply to abide in silence. Because without silence and great practice in letting go of conception, how can we discover what's there beneath all the mental chatter?"

Binita was holding his gaze with a particular intensity. Nodding slowly, she responded with the quote she had been learning, "*There is this city of Brahman and in it …*" she began a little shyly at first, glancing at where his hand was still at his heart, before growing in confidence, "*there is a small shrine in the form of a lotus, and within can be found a small space. This little space within the heart is as great as this vast universe.*"

Across the table, Blake was beaming at her with warm appreciation. "*The heavens and earth are there,*" he continued the quote where she'd left off, to her surprise. Then she joined him, so they were chanting in unison, "*and the sun and the moon and the stars, fire and lightning and wind are there, and all that now is and is not yet – all that is contained within it.*"

After they finished, they held each other's eyes. "The *Chandogya Upanishad,*" Blake confirmed.

"That particular insight," Binita told him, "is my personal talisman."

"I can think of none wiser," he said. "Nor so beautifully expressed."

If such a thing were possible, each of them seemed to have gone up even further in the other's esteem.

"I understand that for Hindus," Blake nodded towards her, "one's purpose in life is to understand the unity of the self, the atman, with Brahman, that space-like bliss consciousness of which everything is a manifestation."

Binita nodded, expression turning pensive.

"This is your journey?"

Her expression clouded. She looked away. "I suppose it is."

Responding to the pause that followed, he asked, "But?"

She looked up eventually, meeting his gaze directly. "The truth is that most of my life has passed me by in a blur of distraction. Growing up. Teenage years. Marriage and children almost completely preoccupied me until my husband's death. My girls and I fell on hard times. It's only recently I've come back to these bigger questions. And when I do, I always ask myself: who am *I* to attain union with Brahman? Most of my life has been quite self-indulgent. I know my flaws, my weaknesses. Is this, seriously, a soul who will attain oneness with God?"

Blake was nodding with a benevolent smile.

"Well," she shrugged. "Is it?"

"Do you really need an answer to that question?"

Sinking against the banquette, her eyes widened. "I don't suppose I do. But it just seems pretty hopeless, knowing it's all beyond me."

"I think," he said eventually, "you may have the right answer but have reached the wrong conclusion."

Bewilderment shadowed Binita's beautiful face.

"A very good friend of mine, Devesh, once explained to me the Hindu concept of two souls," he said. "The outer one, the one you describe as flawed and indulgent. That's our acquired personality, if you like. The being with a biography, with likes and dislikes. *That* soul will not attain oneness with God. No matter how wonderful or terrible, it is discarded at death, just like our body.

"But the inner soul keeps going. It is like a string passing through beads, each bead representing a different life. What we learn on our inner journey, and how we evolve, affects this soul. It makes imprints, positive or negative, which the outer being will experience. But its own nature is pristine. It is completely pure of defilement. *This* is the soul …" Binita's eyes were locked to his as he continued, "that attains oneness with Brahman. *This* is the lotus shrine in the heart as great as the whole universe."

It was as though a burden had been lifted from her shoulders. Binita sat forward in her chair, her expression warm with understanding.

"Thank you," she nodded. "You have no idea how much that lets the light in."

Blake's eyes twinkled.

"Is this what you think?" Her voice was soft. Then with a glint in her eye, "Or do you believe that God really is British?"

He erupted mightily, his laughter booming from the

banquette. "Quite sure of it!" he chuckled. "With a castle and a winged chariot in the Home Counties, in case he ever wants to visit our green and pleasant land!"

After the laughter subsided, he shook his head. "I try steering clear of religion, in general," he said. "You know, the only difference between medicine and poison is the dosage. If religion is a medicine, it should be used with discretion. Use it to heal, to propel growth. But don't become addicted. When we start defining ourselves according to our beliefs, we've really missed the point."

Binita raised her eyebrows.

"That self that wants to be labelled as a 'this' or a 'that', the soul that makes you depressed because it's so flawed or indulged – it's nothing more than a socially acceptable hallucination. If I'm convinced of anything," he leaned across the table, "it's in the importance of abiding in this moment. The eternal here and now. Free from identifying with a self or an I. Free from any thoughts or ideas whatsoever. *That's* where peace is to be found. The field from which all else flows, from which reality emerges. And it's infinite in its peacefulness."

At that moment, Sam stepped down from the bookstore, bringing to the table a copy of the book Blake had requested earlier. As Blake thanked him, Sam asked, "By the way, what was the title of that book by Coleman Barks you recommended?"

Taking out his pen, Sam wrote the title in a small red notebook. He was about to step away when Binita remarked, "Nice pen, Sam."

"Isn't it?" he nodded, holding it out for her to see more

closely. "Given to me by a visitor from Italy yesterday."

"Very generous," observed Blake.

"Truly. His family manufactures them."

As Binita took in the gleaming aquamarine color, the magnificent cap with is gold trim, she recognized she shape of the clip. "Oh! And a cat!"

"Yes."

On cue, they glanced at where I was relaxing on the seat beside her.

"Quite interesting, that," Sam shoved his glasses higher up his nose. "The guy told me that this edition is named after a cat who lived somewhere around here, more than half a century ago. A close companion of his grandparents, apparently. It's called the Luna edition."

"Luna!" Binita's expression was electrifying.

Both men reacted to her expression with curiosity.

Me too, dear reader. How long was it going to take these humans to join the dots?

"And he's Italian?"

He nodded.

"Have you …" her voice lifted with excitement. "Did you tell Serena about this, by any chance?"

"Serena met him."

"Oh."

"Up at Geshe Wangpo's class."

"So," Binita gazed at him intensely. "She knows about the grandparents and the cat called Luna?"

Sam looked pensive, before saying, "Serena had gone home

by the time he mentioned that."

"Sam, we *have* to tell her! And Mrs. Trinci!"

Sam looked startled.

"Is he still in McLeod Ganj? The Italian man? Do you know where he's staying?"

"Flies out tomorrow." Sam was taken aback by the questions. "I think he said The Raj Hotel."

"If this is what it seems to be," Binita looked elated. "You have no idea!" Rising from her seat, she delivered Blake an appreciative expression. "It's been truly wonderful to meet you," she said. "I hope this will be the first conversation of many."

"As do I!" Blake and Sam were both responding to the transformation that had come over her with expressions of gleeful inquiry.

"Now, if you'll excuse me, I must contact Serena immediately!"

Binita left the table, and Sam returned to the bookshop.

"Just you and me together, Dalai Lama's Cat," Blake looked over with a solicitous expression. "May I offer you some milk?"

From the jug beside him, he poured some into a saucer, before reaching under the table and placing it on the floor.

The floor, dear reader! I fixed him with my iciest of blue-eyed stares. How was it possible for such an enlightened being to take such complete leave of his senses?

After a while, as I showed no sign of moving, he got the message. "Oh I see, Miss Puss. Far be it for you to sully your pretty little paws on the ground."

Retrieving the saucer, he placed it on the table. I hopped up with alacrity and, not forgetting my own manners, approached to thank him, lifting my tail to caress his shoulder briefly.

The omniscient Head Waiter Kusali had been following our little exchange. He swooped to the table, smoothly replacing the saucer of milk with a ramekin of clotted cream.

"Rinpoche prefers this," he told Blake, retreating as quickly as he had appeared.

"Rinpoche?" Blake beamed amiably as he repeated the name. "Oh, my dear, you do have them well trained, don't you?"

I paused, contemplating what he'd just said. Was this what made him such a good therapist – seeing things about others that were obvious to him, but weren't at all obvious to them? Or, as in my own case, rarely considered.

Contemplation over, I reached down and began on the cream, with lip-smacking relish.

Blake placed his elbows on the table, resting his chin on his hands, and regarded me genially. "It's been a while since I spent time with a feline friend, Rinpoche," he murmured. "I'm happy to be enjoying this little treat vicariously through you."

I RETURNED HOME SHORTLY AFTER, UP THE STREET TOWARDS the gates of Namgyal Monastery, before starting my way across the courtyard. There was the usual bustle of monks on their way to or from the temple. Groups of tourists being shepherded around in half-a-dozen different languages. Other visitors, gawping or taking photos, or simply absorbing the dream-like image of a Tibetan Buddhist temple set against the backdrop of the soaring snow-capped Himalayas.

As I walked, I saw a middle-aged man in a wheelchair, being supported by a woman of a similar age, I guessed to be his wife, wave down Geshe Wangpo as he was returning from the temple.

"I was hoping to see the Dalai Lama," I heard him say. As I got closer, I saw dark burn marks on his arms and the side of his face.

"He is taking exams today," said Geshe-la.

"Just being in his presence might help Len," implored his wife.

"I'm sorry," shrugged the lama.

Visitors like this were common. People dealing with torment and seeking answers, who hoped for a miraculous encounter.

As Geshe-la continued on his way, Len called out, "Perhaps you can help?"

"Me?" Although Geshe Wangpo was one of the pre-eminent teachers at Namgyal, to this passer-by he was just one of the maroon-clad monastics walking past. Such was Geshe Wangpo's compassion, however, that he paused to hear the man say, "The priest says I am suffering because God's testing me. Why does he say that?"

Geshe Wangpo turned, expression softening. "I am sorry, my friend. You would have to ask him that. Christianity is the business of Christians. Buddhism is the business of Buddhists. It's best not to meddle in each other's business."

"But he makes God sound like a monster!" protested Len.

"Why would he say that?"

"Perhaps," ventured Geshe-la, who was far more knowledgeable about all traditions than he ever let on. "He was trying to help you develop inner strength. Fortitude."

"What would *you* say about me being in an accident that confined me to a wheelchair?" The man wanted to know, in evident despair.

I approached where he and the woman were facing Geshe Wangpo, my arrival catching the lama's eye. If Geshe-la was in any way irked by a distressed man ambushing him with such a tormented existential question, he gave no sign of it. Instead, he met Len's eyes with an expression of calm.

"I don't pretend to know your experience," he said. "But there is one freedom that can never be taken away from us – our freedom of attitude. No person and no circumstances can force us how to think."

Len stared at Geshe Wangpo for a while before saying, "I like that."

The woman was nodding. "Puts you in charge, Len."

"We are always in charge," Geshe-la told them. "Only sometimes we need to be reminded."

"Even when you're trapped in a wheelchair?"

Geshe Wangpo looked at him searchingly for a while, in a way I saw His Holiness sometimes assess visitors, evidently deciding whether or not they were ready to be told something.

"I have many colleagues who choose to go on meditation retreats," he said after a while. "Three years, minimum. Sometimes two or three retreats in a row. A few I know were in retreat for twelve years, came out of retreat – and quickly went back in again!" he chuckled. "Sometimes in a meditation box, not much bigger than a wheelchair. But all of them sitting for four sessions of four hours. Sixteen hours a day. Perfectly still."

Len and his wife both looked flabbergasted.

"They didn't feel trapped. No one was forcing them. What's interesting," Geshe-la raised his hand in emphasis. "Is that when we let go of gross levels of mental activity, of agitation and dullness, when we're able to observe the true nature of our mind, there are no restrictions, no limits. The opposite. The natural state of mind, free from conceptuality, is boundless and radiant and blissful."

Len was following him intently.

"You don't need to be a champion meditator to experience this. We can all have a taste of it. With a little training, a little practice, it becomes more and more our reality when we meditate. Perhaps we come to like it so much, because we find such peace, we want to take our mind there as much as possible. It becomes part of who we are. We integrate it more and more into our thoughts and feelings throughout each day, so that it flows from our sessions into the times in between our sessions.

"If we can train our mind in this way, if this becomes our reality, then what a wonderful thing to have attained, because the subtle mind, the one that leaves this life, is transformed. At the time of death our body closes down, and our gross mind comes to an end too. But subtle consciousness, imprinted by our actions, *this* is what continues."

Len stared at Geshe Wangpo for the longest time before

saying, "Gross mind ends. Subtle mind continues?"

"Yes."

"And all the hurt and pain? This is gross mind?"

The lama was nodding, "Which we let go of."

"You're saying that I should turn my wheelchair into a meditation box?"

"Exactly!"

Hitching himself up in his seat, there seemed a new lightness about Len. I looked up to his wife and she, too, was staring at Geshe-la, astonished. Eyes glistening, Len looked at Geshe Wangpo and said, "You know, I think this is why we came to Dharamshala. I needed to hear this."

The lama was nodding.

"Thank you so much."

"Good, good," Geshe Wangpo had never been the gushy sort, but even he was moved by Len's recognition that his burden might somehow be turned into an opportunity.

Sensing that my time had come, I took a few steps closer, passing the visitors and approaching Geshe-la, weaving between his ankles. After reaching to stroke me, he looked up at Len and his wife. "We can't offer you an audience with the Dalai Lama today," he said. "But I can let you into a little secret."

With a keen sense of dramatic timing, he waited till they were both bending closer towards him. "This is the Dalai Lama's Cat."

"Lord love a duck!" exclaimed Len.

"D'you hear that, Lenny?!" his wife was rapturous.

Not even the revelation of a mind that is boundless and

radiant and not wheelchair-bound, it seemed, could compete – when it came to emotional impact – with my appearance! Soon I was hopping onto Len's lap, his wife wanting to take a photograph, and Geshe Wangpo was excusing himself to return to his rooms.

"Never seen you so thrilled, my love, not since the accident," Len's wife was saying, as she rearranged the wheelchair so that its backdrop was the temple and, in the distance, the mountains with their soaring, glistening summits.

In the late afternoon, the sky above us had lightened from its customary blue to a less certain but softer arc of clarity. And as the enchanted encounter concluded with photographs taken of all three of us, first by Len's wife, then by a young monk, I hoped that what the couple took home with them would be more than what had simply appeared. That along with my fluffy form, sapphire gaze and the knowledge of my famous companion, as we posed together amid the lucid boundlessness, sweeping from one horizon to the other, we were also creating a souvenir of the mind that was beyond conceptuality. A mind that had no thought of wheelchairs or entrapment. A mind with no disquiet about God. A mind that was, instead, simply abiding in whatever this moment gifted, having let go of all concepts and discovering in its place the rapture of the eternal present.

Chapter Seven

After my time in the temple courtyard, I didn't return home to an empty apartment, His Holiness being away in New Delhi overnight. Instead, I was drawn to the garden next door, the one with the lone cedar tree and wooden bench beneath.

What kind of instinct drew me there? Who knows, dear reader? Perhaps I felt in my bones, the way we cats do, that the day's events were far from over and there was more to come. That even if my usual purview – the windowsill overlooking the monastery courtyard – might be a place of cozy familiarity to spend an evening, to go there would be to miss out on an altogether different intrigue.

I ascended the few steps from the sidewalk, arriving in the garden to find a lone figure on the seat. The visitor from Italy was gazing meditatively into the branches of the cedar. I made directly towards him, springing silently to the bench and pausing, inhaling the distinctive mélange of fragrances that shrouded him like an aura. The aromas of faraway vistas of lemons and lavender, of night jasmine clinging to the walls of ancient buildings, of bountiful vineyards and moonlit fountains – all of these were suggested by the ambrosial bouquet emanating from his clothing.

"Ah! Good afternoon, Holy Cat," he greeted me with a certain formality and reverence, glancing from his silent contemplation to find me beside him. "You have come to say goodbye?"

I hadn't, as it happened, being entirely unconcerned by such human conventions.

"It *is* beautiful here, just like Nonna used to say. The snow on the mountains. The magnificent forests. How she must have missed this!"

For a while he continued to look into the distance, as if committing this particular landscape to memory, before reaching out to stroke me all the way from my neck, down my back and along my tail, holding its tip for the briefest moment before letting go. There was a delicacy about his caress, and at the same time an evanescence; much, it seemed, like his visit to Dharamshala.

"We can but try, eh Holy Puss?" he murmured. "I felt such a tug to come out. To see if I could fulfil Nonna's wishes."

It sounded almost confessional. An unburdening of disappointment. "And, I suppose, I hoped that when I came here I might also …" he trailed off. Only after the longest pause he added, "But it was not to be."

I fixed him with an unblinking sapphire-blue stare. I might

not be a telepathist, dear reader, but even I could tell that whatever he was unable to admit was a source of the greatest yearning.

After a few moments, he shifted himself more upright on the bench, straightened his shoulders and shook his head determinedly.

"When I go home," he fixed me with a look of conviction, "I want to be like you. I will find myself a lama and learn at his feet."

It was at that moment that a classic S-type Jaguar pulled into the driveway of the old sanatorium opposite. Coming to a halt, the driver of the car stepped out to check the mailbox set into the right gatepost. It was the same large round bald man with whom I had spent part of that same afternoon. But even if I hadn't seen him for months, I would have recognized him in an instant.

Looking across the road, he offered a characteristically wide and amiable wave.

"Ciao!" responded the visitor.

Blake Ballantyne paused, pressing the bridge of his spectacles to his face with a stubby forefinger. Then he was striding over.

"Italian?" He confirmed, coming closer.

As the visitor nodded, Blake caught sight of me. "And the omnipresent Dalai Lama's Cat," he grunted jocularly, in a way that implied we were already firm friends.

He had reached the bottom of the steps when he said, "This may have nothing to do with you, but are you, by any chance, the fellow who gave a rather nice pen to Sam at the book café?"

The visitor shrugged with nonchalance. "Yes."

Blake soon ascended the steps, hand outstretched in greeting. "Blake Ballantyne!" he said. "You don't know me, but I've just come from the café. There's a lot of excited talk about you down there, concerning your grandfather."

"Grandfather?" The other man was suddenly animated.

Blake pulled a phone out of his pocket. "Exactly," he responded, a glint in his eye.

Within minutes, Sid had pulled up across the road in his silver SUV, accompanied by Serena and Mrs. Trinci, Rishi having been left at home with his nanny. As they were getting out of the car, Sam appeared on foot from the opposite direction, out of breath from his exertions. Before they'd even crossed the road, Mrs. Trinci was calling out something in Italian. The visitor responded accordingly, before Serena chastised her mother about speaking a foreign language in the company of those who did not. Mrs. Trinci wailed her apologies operatically as she crossed the road, bangles clashing about her arms, ascending the steps as though onto a stage.

Introductions were quickly performed, Mrs. Trinci describing herself as a long-term resident of Dharamshala, originally from Italy's Amalfi Coast. Lorenzo Conti, as our visitor was named, responded that he knew that part of the world very well, spending months there every year. Serena and Sid had little time to say much, beyond the fact that they lived nearby. Lorenzo, at everyone's insistence, resumed his seat beside me,

Mrs. Trinci sat next to us and Serena perched on the other side of Lorenzo. As the late-afternoon rays lengthened, Sam, Sid and Blake eased themselves onto the lawn. Slipping in behind the three of them, unnoticed in the commotion, was Binita.

The anticipation at that moment could hardly have been any greater. But where to start? And with whom? Mrs. Trinci reached over to clutch Lorenzo's arm, fumbling as she did and ending up squeezing his leg awkwardly instead. As the Maharajah of Himachal Pradesh, Sid might have been expected to open the conversation. But ever the diplomat, he deferred to Sam, who had been more directly involved in what had gone before. Sam, in turn, deferred to Serena.

Which is how it fell to outgoing Blake, the newcomer who had had the least to do with any of this, but in the shortest time had surmised its importance to everyone, to begin.

"I know that you all wanted to speak to Lorenzo before he leaves tomorrow," he said, glancing around at the eager faces. "Having made the connection between him and his grandfather."

"And I ..." Lorenzo declared, "have been doing all I could to find out from the authorities about Nonno and where he is buried. But," he glanced at Sam shrugging, "nothing."

"The pen." Sam withdrew it from his jacket pocket and held it towards him. "Named after your Nonno's cat, Luna?"

"Yes." Lorenzo's eyes burned with a bright intensity, as he looked around at their faces. "But how do *you* know about my grandfather?"

"*I* don't," replied Sam. "You told me about a cat called Luna

131

who lived with your grandparents, when you gave me the pen."

Lorenzo was nodding.

"I didn't make the connection. Not on my own. But I had heard before about an Italian priest who lived in the mountains and used to have a cat."

Lorenzo looked baffled and eager in equal measure.

"Let me show you something." Mrs. Trinci's eyes glistened as she opened the clasp of her handbag and reached inside, retrieving the small metal plate that had been hidden for so long. She handed it to him.

"Qui giacciono le spoglie mortali di Luna, la gatta prediletta di Padre Lorenzo." He read aloud, emotion rapidly taking hold of him, so that by the time he'd finished, his voice was barely a whisper. *"Requiescat in pace."*

His eyes filling with emotion, he looked from the plaque to Mrs. Trinci. "Where did you find this?" he managed eventually.

"In our garden," she spoke softly. "Actually," she looked down, stroking my neck, "it was this little one who found it. She went exploring under the bushes."

"The Dalai Lama's Cat found Luna's inscription?" The profound sentiment welling up inside him was laced with an expression of incredulity.

"Sì."

"And you live in the same place as Nonno ... but wasn't it destroyed by fire?"

"Yes." On the other side of him, Serena confirmed, "The cottage was destroyed. There was very little left – just a pile of rubble. Sid and I," she gestured to her husband, "didn't know it had ever been there. It was on our property, you see, at the far end of the lawn under a great tangle of bougainvillea. But one day we went exploring and realized that someone used to live there."

"When you went exploring," the visitor interjected, an urgency filling his eyes, "did you find something?"

"Your Nonno's garden," Serena told him.

"I mean a grave. A tomb. A place of burial?"

She was shaking her head. "Nothing like that," she said. "But the garden your grandfather established was so beautifully mature, it was the perfect place to build a new home for my mother. There was one thing in particular that drew us. That enchanted Mamma …"

"His tree!" Mrs. Trinci could contain herself no longer, fluttering her heavily darkened eyelashes demonstrably.

Lorenzo's expression was blank. "Tree?"

"The Italian stone pine he brought from home," prompted Serena.

Staring into the distance, Lorenzo searched among ancient memories for some half-forgotten scrap of conversation. "He took out many seedlings," he spoke eventually in a faraway voice, recalling what he'd been told. "Only two survived."

"Two?" confirmed Mrs. Trinci.

"*Si. Si.* I think this is what Nonna said," he murmured. Then after a pause, "I had forgotten this, about Nonno. That he brought his precious trees with him from Italy."

"A dendrophile. Like you," said geeky Sam from the lawn in front of him. "*The Myth of Trees,*" he reminded him of his recent purchase.

"A book I had been searching for over many years," Lorenzo was fervent. "And do you know why? Because the author was a dear friend of my Nonno's. He even visited him here in Dharamshala once. And he kept in touch with Nonna all the years she was in Italy. He used to come to the house when I was a boy."

"You see, we didn't know this …" Serena began, "that your Nonna moved to Italy. There's so much we don't know about your family."

"Which feels so very close to ours," Mrs. Trinci was emphatic. "Even living in the same place!"

It did seem that the most curious and profound connections were being revealed, patterns of influence reverberating through the generations, assuming a magical significance in the velvet twilight. The dance of India and Italy, of love and loss, of matter and spirit were the most obvious manifestations. But there seemed more to it than what was apparent. In that small garden, the yearning for wholeness felt as perceptible as the evening breeze.

Lorenzo was looking directly at Sam. "You didn't make the connection," he queried after a long while, "between the pen and my grandfather?"

Sam nodded.

"Who did?"

There was a pause, before Sam and Blake both turned to look over their shoulders.

Between the two of them, Binita rose to her feet. With her

turquoise sari, elegant features and munificent gaze, she may have seemed to Lorenzo, at that moment, more like a vision than reality. Like a deity arising, who was lifting him to his feet too.

"It was me," she said, through the lengthening shadows.

Eyes fixed, he stepped towards her.

There are rare moments, dear reader, when two beings become so completely absorbed by one another that they have no awareness of anything else. Time and self-awareness fall away, as each focuses with utter enthrallment on the other. This was one of those moments. Lorenzo and Binita stepped towards each other with what felt like a cosmic inevitability. A force as powerful as the drawing together, in former times, of Padre Lorenzo and his spiritual soulmate, Uma. Lorenzo's hazel eyes as transfixed on Binita as hers were on him. Lost in each other.

Acknowledging the intimacy of the moment, Sid was the first to get up from the grass and dust off his knees. Somewhat self-consciously, Blake and Sam followed suit, approaching where Serena and Mrs. Trinci were getting off the bench seat.

"I'll be on my way," Blake spoke softly and was immediately seconded by Sam. "But I am most intrigued to hear the rest of the story." He gestured towards where Lorenzo was taking Binita's hands in his own.

It was only when Blake and Sam had stepped from the garden onto the pavement and were walking away that Lorenzo and Binita turned to the others. "What now?" asked Lorenzo.

Sid walked over and placed a hand on each of their shoulders. "You're joining us for dinner," he commanded. "At home.

There is much to discuss."

"There is," agreed Lorenzo.

"We'll walk," said Binita – meaning Lorenzo and her.

"Of course," Sid stepped away.

In a short while, I was being clutched by Mrs. Trinci to her ample bosom, as she made her way towards Sid's SUV. His Holiness wasn't at home tonight, she told her daughter and son-in-law, in a tone that brooked no dissent. And besides, none of this would be happening were it not for The Most Beautiful Creature That Ever Lived. I was coming to dinner with them too.

"Wow!" Serena was the first to speak once we were all in the car; Sid reversed into the old sanatorium driveway, before turning the car in the direction away from town. "What was that about?!"

"Karma," declared Mrs. Trinci.

"As it's rarely seen," agreed Sid.

"Was that how you felt when you first saw me?" Serena teased her husband.

"Naturally!" he returned, with a wry smile.

"The whole story!" crooned Mrs. Trinci, processing what they'd just heard. "Uma went to Italy and had a child. I wonder what it was like for her, living in Europe?"

"And did she ever return to India?" questioned Serena. "I also wonder about Lorenzo and how alike he seems to his Nonno." After a pause she continued, "What if he *is* the continuity of his grandfather – his mindstream, I mean?"

She glanced, for a response, towards Sid behind the steering wheel.

"Perhaps," he shrugged. "It's said that if we feel great attachment to certain people or places, we can be drawn back to them. Sometimes that means returning to the same family."

"But Binita couldn't be Uma," Serena was working through the timeline. "Or could she?"

"Whatever is playing out," nodded Sid. "It is the most powerful karma. Very strong attachment." Before observing after a while, "Whenever we find ourselves immediately drawn to a stranger or repelled by them in a way we cannot fathom, chances are it's past-life stuff."

"Amazing to think how many connections we have with others from our past lives," observed Serena.

"My little green book!" exclaimed Mrs. Trinci from the back.

For as long as I'd known her, she had carried it in her handbag. Compact, sturdy, with a worn cloth cover and brass-colored clasp, it contained the contact details of family, friends and catering suppliers. She used it less these days, with so many names already in her phone. But she always brought it with her. "It has dozens of names in it. Maybe hundreds."

"I'd say hundreds, Mamma!" Serena chuckled from the passenger seat.

"Many of them, dear friends. In some cases, still in my life. In others, we were together for only a season. But still – there was a connection."

She was silent for a while. "What if I had the same thing in my last life? The equivalent of all those people in my green book? And the life before that one? And before that one, and before that one?"

"All the way back to the beginning of time," offered Sid.

"Exactly," agreed Mrs. Trinci. "Where are all those people now?"

"Some of them in your life today, but in different guises," replied Sid. "Sometimes friends, sometimes lovers, sometimes people you don't like…"

"Cats," proposed Mrs. Trinci, kissing me appreciatively.

"Of course," laughed Serena.

"And most importantly of all," Sid was wagging his index finger, "mothers!"

"*Si!*" His own mother-in-law agreed emphatically.

"Important because they give us life. Take care of us when we are in greatest need."

"But from what you just said," Mrs. Trinci wanted to go back a few steps. "People who we don't like. Enemies from our past lives. They could be around us too?"

"Of course."

"So why does the *Dharma* tell us to treat all beings like they were our mothers from a previous lifetime? What if some people once did us great harm?"

"Ah," smiled Sid. "That's the difference between an antidote and a truth."

"Go on," demanded Mrs. Trinci.

"An antidote helps us cultivate a state of mind that's useful for inner growth. The *Dharma* is full of antidotes. Opponent practices."

I was reminded how Serena used the same term, when she'd met with Binita in the gardens of The Sukhavati Spa. How she had told Binita to find a mental treasure, a protective amulet, something that gave her genuine joy to contemplate when she found herself sinking into a slough of despondency.

"For example," Sid was saying. "Instead of treating someone who always irritates us like a pain in the backside, we reframe them as our Precious Treasure, because they can help us cultivate that most valuable quality of patience – something that our friends rarely do."

Mrs. Trinci was nodding, familiar with this notion.

"That's an antidote," continued Sid. "Because it helps us to use the situation we're in to develop a more powerful mind, instead of just getting angry."

"*Si, si.*"

"It's the same with the people around us. They *may* have been our mothers in a previous lifetime. Not being clairvoyant, we don't know that for a fact. But adopting that view helps us avoid being indifferent to strangers. It's a form of mind training, that makes it easier for us to cultivate our compassion."

Serena was pensive. "Of course, not everyone has the kind of relationship that we do, Mamma. In which case, we could think of others as having been our dearest friend. Our lover. Someone to whom we were especially close. There are so many possibilities."

"*Si,*" agreed her mother. "A whole little green book of

possibilities. But some of them have passed away. And others," she shrugged. "Who knows where they are? We lost touch."

"But you still remember them?"

"Of course! Some of them made … a very big impact," she chuckled.

"Even though the relationship has passed," observed Sid. "There is still an imprint. One that will play out in the future. Positive or negative."

"I suppose we must do all we can," mused Serena, "to leave things as positively as possible in every relationship. From our side, at least."

"That's true," agreed Sid. "We do whatever we can, but what other people think is outside our control."

"What about imprints from people we've never met, but where there are strong feelings?" Mrs. Trinci wanted to know. "Like politicians?"

Sid shrugged. "Same thing. We may believe their policies are wrong, or dislike how they behave. There may be some high-profile criminal case, where someone's found guilty of an appalling crime. But if we buy into the hate, the vengeance, the nastiness, then we've just created a negative imprint in our own mindstream, because of a complete stranger."

For a while, everyone in the vehicle digested this awkward recognition. How much future unhappiness had been created because of animosity towards a human, or other being, who we had never even met?

After a pause, Mrs. Trinci asked Sid, "You said there is a difference between an antidote and a truth. So, what would be a truth?"

"In a situation where we're wanting to cultivate equanimity," he replied, "a truth would be that all beings are just the same as us, in wishing for happiness and to avoid suffering."

"A different way to help develop compassion," she confirmed, "instead of thinking about all beings as having been our mother."

Sid nodded, as he indicated left and slowed to turn into the driveway of their home. "Of course, Buddha's ultimate truth," he murmured, "is *shunyata*. The way that things exist. Once we have some understanding of this, even just as an idea, we begin to see everything quite differently."

Three things cannot be hidden for long, dear reader: the sun, the moon and the truth. Wasn't it a wise sage who said this? The Dalai Lama perhaps, or even Buddha himself? At my age, attributing all the percipient things one has heard to the correct source can be exhausting. Suffice to say that whatever had been hidden about Padre Lorenzo, Uma and all that had followed, it was to be fully revealed that evening. In the room at the top of the tower in Sid and Serena's home, a chamber with the most panoramic of vistas, it was as though the past was shown to us with all the clarity of the surrounding countryside.

Lorenzo and Binita appeared on the drive a short time later, engrossed in conversation. By then, Serena, Mrs. Trinci and I were upstairs, Serena having lit candles in ornate gold tea-light holders and put on a playlist of soothing ambient music. Sid met the couple in the hallway and guided them up to join us.

It was Lorenzo's first visit to the property and he was entranced. He stepped into the tower room, which felt like it was suspended in the afterglow of sunset on the Himalayas, the melting icecaps red as cerise in the setting sun. After he'd had time to take in the mesmerizing splendor, Binita showed him to the window opposite.

"That's the rebuilt cottage," she pointed to Mrs. Trinci's home in the distance. "And behind it, the garden. And at the end of the garden …"

"The stone pine from Amalfi," he finished in barely a whisper, before turning to the others, his light hazel eyes brimming with emotion.

"Come, come," sinking onto a sofa, Mrs. Trinci patted the seat next to hers. "We want to know everything."

After they were settled with drinks, Mrs. Trinci, Lorenzo and I sharing one sofa, Sid and Serena sitting opposite, and Binita perched on a brocade pouffe next to our special guest, Lorenzo told us his story. He filled the gaps in a tale which had been veiled in enigma for over half a century.

All those years ago after Lorenzo Conti, former priest, had been killed in the fire, his wife Uma had remained in McLeod Ganj only long enough to arrange his funeral and burial. Then she had hastily left. She truly had no idea who had set fire to their little home, said Lorenzo, or what motivated them. She never found out. All she knew was that the same people who had murdered her husband may have wanted to kill her too.

Once she reached New Delhi, Lorenzo's distraught parents, who she'd never met, invited her to visit them in Italy. In the absence of other plans and with little money, she had accepted their invitation and was warmly received by the whole Conti clan. When she discovered that she was pregnant, she was persuaded to stay at the ancestral villa near Florence, until she gave birth to a son who she named Paolo. He, in turn, became the father of the Lorenzo sitting with us.

From the moment Paolo was born, Uma's father-in-law, Tommaso Conti, tried his utmost to keep Uma and the new baby in Italy. Founder of a family-owned pen-making business and a successful businessman with dynastic ambitions, he had a vision of his company continuing through the generations to become one of Italy's most prestigious manufacturers of writing instruments. For that he required heirs.

Initially, Uma had needed little persuasion to keep away from India, being deterred by fear. Finding her feet in the new world and coming to understand how devoted Tommaso was to his grandson, she recognized how karma was propelling her down an unexpected path, although she still used to talk about returning home. An intensely spiritual woman of few needs, when the family acquired a small holiday house in Ravello, on the Amalfi Coast, Uma felt powerfully drawn to it and made it her own.

She never remarried. Lorenzo had been her one true love. When tragedy struck the Conti family yet again, and her late husband's only brother was killed in a motorbike accident, little Paolo became the sole successor to the family business. Uma stopped talking about a return to India.

Paolo had been his grandfather's child – loyal, energetic and with an endless capacity for hard work. Growing up to marry a beautiful Venetian girl and become the father of three children, he had also more than fulfilled Tommaso's business ambitions, expanding distribution of the family firm's prestigious writing instruments worldwide.

Lorenzo's older brother, Giovanni, had followed in his father's footsteps. Their young sister, Marina, was the family beauty. Lorenzo, the second son, was more like the grandfather he had never met, according to all who had known Padre Lorenzo. And he'd had a special relationship with Uma, spending holidays with her on the Amalfi Coast, loving the stories she used to tell him about his Nonno, the mystic, adventurer and dreamer who had gone out to India.

It was Nonna Uma who had taught him how to meditate. They'd sit together on the balcony of her Ravello home, breathing in the scent of the pine trees, as they gazed out towards the endless cobalt sweep of the Mediterranean, in a state of abiding peace.

"Of the three grandchildren, I was always closest to Nonna," Lorenzo said now. "And through her I felt this connection to India, a feeling of familiarity, even though I had never been here. I knew what it meant to her and Nonno. How it was a place of transcendent possibilities. Somewhere for a spiritual traveler to come home."

In the radiance of the tower room, it was as if each one of us was now an intimate of the Conti family. We had taken

Lorenzo to our hearts, and he had taken us to his. The story of Father Lorenzo and Uma, a drama which had played out on this very property, had become part of our own shared history, their place in our part of the world now connected to him.

After meeting the eyes of the small group, his own gaze fell to the ground. "Last year in January, Nonna died," he said. "Then my father also, later in the summer. Two hammer blows to our family in one calendar year."

Mrs. Trinci reached out instinctively to comfort him.

"Giovanni, my brother, who eats and sleeps and breathes the business, had to step into father's shoes quickly. He has been overwhelmed with work. I, on the other hand," he shrugged, "am less commercially inclined. I have been taking care of family matters. Father's estate, which is complicated. Disposing of Nonna's few things.

"Father's death was sudden, a heart attack. He hadn't seen to Nonna's ashes when he died. Nonna had always told us she didn't care what happened to her remains. I found her small casket in his home office. I thought he had been strangely hesitant about disposing of them, which wasn't like my father.

"Then I was going through Nonna's own few papers. That is where I found a note she had written, years earlier, saying that she'd like her remains to be buried alongside her husband's." Lorenzo looked up. "That was when I knew what had held my father back. On some level, I think she wanted to be reunited with India, with Lorenzo, even if only as a symbol. Father knew this too. He may have been planning to visit McLeod Ganj to carry out her wishes."

"This is why you asked earlier!" Mrs. Trinci exclaimed. "About a grave?"

"*Si.*"

"You thought he might be buried here?"

"Yes," Lorenzo's face filled with anguish, as he looked at her. "I can't be sure, but I think Nonna once told me that Nonno was buried in the forest, not far from the cottage. I so wished I had asked her when I had the chance. Got her to tell me *exactly* where it was. But you see, I didn't know anything about her wanting to be interred with him. Not until after she died." He was shaking his head before saying, "Anyway, if Nonno's grave was there," he looked at Serena and Sid, "you would have found it by now."

Serena turned to Sid with a probing expression.

"I can see why the bureaucrats were confused by my questions," Lorenzo turned back to Binita. "I was asking them about a person for whom they had no record, in a grave that isn't marked."

There was a pause before Sid spoke, his voice lucid and commanding as ever, that soft Indian accent with an undertow of the Raj. But in the flow of it, the hint of a promise. "There's just a couple of things I would say," he spoke softly. "We *haven't* found a grave. That much is true. But nor have we ever looked for one. We didn't know that a grave might be there."

"Mum's garden – your Nonno's garden – flows directly into the forest." Serena was explaining. "It is so dense, so thick, that we seldom walk in there. We've never properly explored it."

The sun had slipped completely behind the horizon and the

only natural light coming into the room was reflected by the icy caps of the mountains – now an impossible, glistening pink. And a new look had come into Lorenzo's eyes. A lightness, arising from the entirely unexpected resurrection of hope.

"You said a couple of things?" he looked over, prompting Sid.

Sid nodded. "When we bought the property, there was no reference to a grave on the report given to me by the surveyor," his voice was calm. "But I do remember him saying that there had been talk of a shrine on the land. He had lived in these parts for many years, the surveyor. Back then, our main interest was making sure we could build our home here. But what if the shrine was perhaps a headstone? And not from ancient times? It's not impossible that Padre Lorenzo's grave could be somewhere here."

Lorenzo stood, turned and gazed across the pink terraces to where the windows of Mrs. Trinci's cottage glowed brightly in the deepening shadows. Behind it, the small lamplit garden led all the way to where that living icon of Padre Lorenzo himself soared skywards, arms stretching through the darkness.

"I thought my visit here was over," Lorenzo's voice was quiet. "I thought I had done what I could. That there was nothing left for me. My suitcase is packed – just about. I was going to spend this evening alone in my hotel room reading. But instead …" turning back to face the group, his eyes immediately met Binita's. "All this!"

Binita reached out, drawing him back to where he had been sitting, the entreaty in her eyes as fierce as his own brooding intensity. As he glanced back at Sid, his host told him, "It would be easy enough to arrange a proper search in the daylight."

Lorenzo was nodding, thoughtfully.

Then Serena said, "A friend of ours works in travel. What if we could reschedule your flight?"

Back on my windowsill later that night, as I looked over the moonlit courtyard of the monastery, I remembered the effect on Lorenzo of seeing Binita for the first time. How Sid had later recalled the well-known teaching that, through attachment, we are drawn back to certain people or places for lifetime after lifetime.

I thought of Mrs. Trinci and her little green book. Had my own name been listed in this hypothetical compendium in one of her recent lifetimes? If so, what had my name been? And, for that matter, hers? Did this explain our particularly close connection in this life, beyond my obvious gluttony?

Some years ago, it had been revealed to me how I'd come to find myself in the home of His Holiness. Deeply disconcerting as the idea had been, I discovered that in a previous lifetime I had actually been the Dalai Lama's dog! It was certainly no spiritual attainments on my own part that had led me back to his inner sanctum in a more elevated feline form – rather, my attachment to him was what had done it. Just like Sid said, our attachments and aversions, carried along in our stream of consciousness, are what propel us into future experiences. They are why things appear to us the way they do. The claw of attraction.

And that night, as I rested my head on my paws and closed my eyes, Sid's observation that you don't even have to know someone personally for attachments or aversions to be created, gave rise to the most intriguing recognition. One which concerns not only me, dear reader, but more importantly, you.

The Dalai Lama may be a human you have personally never met, or perhaps seen only briefly or from a distance. As for me, unless you have had the good fortune of dining at The Himalaya Book Café, visiting Namgyal Monastery at just the right moment, or attending sound healing at The Sukhavati Spa, the most you will ever have seen of me is the bewitching sweep of a luxuriant grey tail, while watching a Zoom teaching by His Holiness.

And yet despite all this, we have a connection, you and I, do we not? Attachments have been formed. Imprints of the most auspicious kind have been created. The causes not only for us to connect again in the future, but for you to meet with the *Dharma*. With extraordinary holy beings. Perhaps even with His Holiness himself – whatever his manifestation?

May love, compassion, joy and equanimity pervade the hearts and minds of all limitless beings throughout universal space. This was my final thought that night, as all nights, before willing myself to my own personal heaven, that other Sukhavati, home of Amitabha, the Buddha of Infinite Light.

CHAPTER EIGHT

ARE YOU A SPY, DEAR READER? NOT OF THE CLANDESTINE national secrets variety – although if you are, how very intriguing! My whiskers tingle at the prospect that my readers may include someone engaged in a surreptitious double life. Nor do I mean a spy of the nosy-neighbor type, overly interested in humdrum activities going on next door.

No, the spy to whom I refer is of the Buddhist kind, not only approved but actively encouraged. The sort of being who always keeps a vigilant watch on their every thought. Engaged in round-the-clock surveillance of mind itself.

Of course, lamas don't talk about spying. At least, not usually. The term they use instead is 'introspective awareness' or, even more plainly, 'mindfulness of mind'. But it is the same thing, no? Scrutinizing a target who usually goes about its business unobserved. Seeing what it does and where its activities lead. Becoming aware of its every habit and foible. So deepening one's familiarity with its actions – in particular those that diverge from what might be preferred – that over time, the simple act of observation begins to change what is observed.

My own inner espionage, like most things I do, is sporadic. But one thought that did seem to be sticking was my inner amulet. The treasure of the mind I had chosen for myself on that afternoon when Serena had counselled Binita in the garden at The Sukhavati Spa : *How lucky I am to be the Dalai Lama's Cat!* I had made this thought my own quite spontaneously. Then deliberately recollected it in the days and weeks that followed. It was, after all, so real. So true. A thought I could entertain with effortless joy.

Curiously, after making a point of invoking the amulet for several weeks, I had discovered it had begun to recur quite of its own accord. I might be gazing across the Namgyal courtyard, or grooming myself in the sunshine next door, or pausing for an instant on my way down the road to The Himalaya Book Café, when it would suddenly bubble up in my mind: *How lucky I am to be the Dalai Lama's Cat.* Ah yes, my inner spy observes. Here comes that thought again – and this time without deliberation. Unplanned. And along with the thought, something else. Something I should perhaps have expected, but didn't. Something, dear reader, that came as a quite delightful surprise.

How lucky I am to be the Dalai Lama's Cat. The thought resurfaced as I hopped downstairs, along the outside ledge of the building, the morning after Lorenzo's momentous revelations – and his convergence with Binita. I'd woken that morning in time for our usual 4 am meditation start and remembered that the Dalai Lama was visiting New Delhi. I had, nonetheless, occupied my usual place on the meditation mat, with the very best of intentions. Alas, sleep overcame me. Without the presence of His Holiness, instead of clarity and light, I soon felt overwhelmed by a dull cloudiness. By the time I woke, the building was already abuzz with activity.

Down in the kitchen, Mrs. Trinci was preparing a few dishes for the lunch the Dalai Lama would be hosting the following day. As always, the warm aroma of baking wafted from the humming ovens, as she also prepared a few home-baked treats for his staff. And, it turned out, the search party that Sid had assembled. As she moved about the kitchen preparing several different dishes at once, she was also telling Oliver all about the evening before.

Having left Sid and Serena's home just after nightfall, I had missed out on what happened after Serena offered to see whether Lorenzo's flight home to Italy could be rescheduled. It seemed that had been achieved, from the way Mrs. Trinci was explaining things to His Holiness's Executive Assistant, who was perched on a kitchen stool nibbling a madeleine, fresh from the oven.

Last night, Sid had arranged a search party to help look for Padre Lorenzo's grave. Staff from home and The Sukhavati Spa, as well as friends, neighbors and a couple of people from the local history association, were due to meet up the road in the next half hour. Sid and Lorenzo had studied a map of the estate over dinner the night before, deciding how best to conduct the search. As soon as she had finished her prep work, Mrs. Trinci told Oliver, she would be returning home to help with the search – and provide midmorning refreshments.

Scooping me up enthusiastically the moment she saw me arrive, Mrs. Trinci was soon serving me my own refreshments on the kitchen table, as Oliver went upstairs to begin his working day. I munched lustily from the saucer of tender tuna with cheese sauce, as Mrs. Trinci bustled about the kitchen singing Nat King Cole songs under her breath, the way she always did when she was bright with expectation.

How lucky I am to be the Dalai Lama's Cat I thought, as I finished my meal. Raising my head from the empty saucer, I looked appreciatively about me, then gave my paw a generous tuna-coated lick, before washing behind my ears.

"When I fall in love," Mrs. Trinci was warbling, almost in tune but not quite. "It will be …"

"Mamma!" Serena appeared suddenly at the kitchen door. I hadn't heard her car arrive above the kitchen noises. "They found it!"

"What?"

"The grave!" Her eyes were filled with exultation.

Mrs. Trinci glanced at the digital clock on the oven. "But it's not even 10 am!"

"A few of us went at first light," Serena told her. "Sid, Lorenzo, Binita and I. A couple of staff."

"Is it near my house?" Mrs. Trinci's eyes gleamed with

excitement.

"You know that path we sometimes take along the side of your property? That they used to bring in the lawn?"

"*Sì.*"

"Where it carries on down the side of the mountain …"

"Round the curve," interjected Mrs. Trinci.

"Just after the curve," Serena told her. "That's where it is."

"On the right?" she queried.

Serena shook her head. "Left."

"But there's no space on the left. Just rock. Creepers."

"Which is why we have always walked past it. We always thought it was just a bank of rock. Which it is. But if you clear away the plants, you see the grave was dug into it." Serena was pulling her phone out of her pocket, to show her mother a photo.

Donning her glasses, Mrs. Trinci peered at the screen. "Very well hidden!"

"Nonna made sure of it," agreed Serena.

"How did you find it?"

"It was Binita, actually. She was looking for something different from the rest of us."

Mrs. Trinci fixed her mascara-lashed eyes on her inquisitively.

"*We* were looking on the ground, brushing away leaves and branches, searching for a gravestone, a marker of some kind. Binita told us afterwards she was also looking up at the trees. She had this theory about umbrella pines. Remember how Lorenzo told us, last night, that two of Father Lorenzo's saplings had survived?"

"*Si.*"

"We knew one was in your garden. Binita's idea was that the grave might be beside the other one," said Serena. "Turns out she was right."

"There is another pine in the forest?"

"Just like yours – tall and straight," Serena confirmed. "Directly above the grave, among a whole lot of other plants. Not something you'd notice, unless you were looking for it. It would have been just a small tree when they buried Lorenzo's Nonno. But now ..."

"The roots go down?"

"Exactly. To where he was buried."

"And this?" Mrs. Trinci was pointing to the screen. "What does it say?"

"*Here lies a half of my soul,*" read Serena. "And his name: *Lorenzo Conti, 4 October 1913 – 18 April 1959.*"

"I know how Uma felt. That she'd lost half of herself," Mrs. Trinci was uncharacteristically mournful for a moment. As she empathized with the widow she'd heard so much about, I thought how Mrs. Trinci herself had been a widow for as long as I'd known her. "And so very young."

Serena wrapped her arms around her mother, and for a moment they hugged.

Then Mrs. Trinci said into Serena's shoulder, "Now Lorenzo can fulfil his Nonna's wishes."

"Yes," agreed Serena, as they broke apart. "Sid has already given Lorenzo his approval to inter her remains next to the

Padre's. They want to do something small but appropriate. Decide what words to put on the headstone."

Mrs. Trinci was pensive. "Perhaps what each of them found truly inspiring?"

"There was a bit of talk about that," said Serena. "According to Uma, the things that drew Father Lorenzo to Buddhism, more than anything, was *bodhichitta*."

"Ah, yes!"

"She said that, in his last years, it was what caused him to withdraw from the world. To focus on meditation and insight."

"I see."

As an alarm sounded, Mrs. Trinci turned towards the oven from whence it came. "Now …" she demanded, her mercurial features quickly changing, "what am I to do with all this food?!

I had the day to fill before the Dalai Lama was due to arrive back in the late evening. So I followed what had become my customary routine: the morning at Namgyal, much of it sprawled on top of the filing cabinet in the Executive Assistants' office, followed by lunch and a siesta at The Himalaya Book Café. I was contemplating a visit to The Sukavati Spa that afternoon, but I heard Franc mention something about going to The Downward Dog School of Yoga later that afternoon. It was a very long time since I had observed a class there and attended one of the post-class sessions on the balcony that looked directly to the mountains. Time, I decided, to make a return.

Trailing Franc and Heidi, who left the café together in their bamboo yoga clothes, rolled mats under their arms, I followed them up the steep hill to the modest bungalow where Ludwig had always held his classes. It was all reassuringly unchanged: the same sign in faded lettering, the small hallway with a shoe rack filled with footwear. The beaded curtain which led to the very large room facing a panoramic vista of the Himalayas. Bi-fold doors running the whole length of the room were pushed back and beyond the doors was the balcony, the gathering place for post-class tea and discussions, which sometimes lasted until long after nightfall.

In this place, the mountains seemed somehow so extraordinarily close that if you reached your paw out far enough, you could almost touch them. When you were at The Downward Dog School of Yoga, you felt that you were communing directly with the mountains. Moving in their presence. Breathing in their pristine air. Gently lifted out of your usual state of being, to a state that was more transcendent and peaceful, simply by being here.

The Downward Dog School of Yoga had been set up in the 1960s by a young German man, Ludwig – or Ludo – who had come to Dharamshala at the express invitation of his friend, Heinrich Harrer, of *Seven Years in Tibet* fame. In those days, the Dalai Lama and his entourage had only recently arrived. Ludo had soon met him and a bond between the two had formed, so that when I was with Ludo, I knew that I was with a friend too. A rigorous and disciplined yoga teacher of the old school, Ludo was now in his 80s. Visiting Germany several years earlier, he had returned with his niece Heidi, also a yoga teacher, who he had planned to succeed him. But there'd been a clash over her broader, more eclectic style. She had stayed in town, become involved with Ricardo, the handsome Colombian barista at the café, and was now running group classes at The Sukhavati Spa. Although Ludo and Heidi had patched up their differences, Ludo continued as the sole teacher at his studio, his tanned features and white hair somehow timeless, his blue eyes as vibrant as when they'd first met my own aquamarine gaze.

That evening's class followed the same entirely predictable routine that his classes always did. That was the point of them. They comprised a set of movements and asanas that were comprehensive in their invigorating effects – for which Ludwig himself provided glowing testimony. I watched the yogis from my usual purview at the back. All the regulars were present: Sid and Serena – who had first met right here; Franc from the café; Ewing the piano-playing American; and Heidi, who still found time from her work at the nearby spa to attend her uncle's classes.

There was a closeness among them, having practiced in this same place for many years. From start to finish, it was a familiar, but always subtly different journey they made together. After lying for some time in *shavasana*, they would rise from their mats, venture onto the deck, and gather in the sunset to sip green tea from beakers.

The balcony was lined with handwoven rugs and furnished with bean bags, cushions and bolsters. It wasn't long before they were gathered around Ludo, facing each other and I along with them, settling on a faded amber pouffe between Ludo and Serena. Talk soon turned to the tale of Lorenzo Conti, the handsome stranger from Italy, who had come to Dharamshala on a mission to find his grandfather's grave – or for that matter, any reference to his grandfather. And how, on the eve of departing from a fruitless visit, things had dramatically changed.

Franc and some of the café regulars knew most of the story. Others were quickly brought up to date. Serena shared the news of that morning – how Padre Lorenzo's grave, unknown and overlooked for so long, had been rediscovered. And how his grandson planned to inter the Padre's late wife's remains alongside his. It was a story of curious coincidence, with a heartwarming denouement, and the yogis on the balcony were engrossed by it.

As the mountains above enacted their own nightly ritual, icy caps reflecting the colors of the sun, beginning with golden butter-yellow, there was conversation about Lorenzo junior and the similarities he shared with his grandfather. How brave Padre Lorenzo had been for his day, shedding the security of Europe to venture out to India. And then, on discovering the wealth of spiritual riches to be found here, forsaking even the safety of the priesthood, of all he had known, to strike out on his own journey.

"He was a pioneer!" exclaimed Merrilee, often strident in her views. "A trailblazer for us Western seekers who come to India."

"Although," Sid pointed out, "he was a finder more than a seeker."

"Yes," agreed Serena. "Quite settled in his beliefs when he arrived. But not an easy man. Volatile and prickly, we hear."

The group digested this in silence before Heidi said, "I wonder what it was that so inspired him to change, after he got here?"

"Or who?" Merrilee grinned mischievously.

"Or both," proposed Ewing, taking a sip from his beaker.

Serena was nodding. "Lorenzo told us this morning that his Nonna used to say it was *bodhichitta* which he found the most sublime motivation. He had never come across anything like it before."

"Ah," sighed Franc. Heads were nodding.

"It's entirely possible," Serena continued, glancing towards Merrilee. "That he found in Uma a manifestation of that same quality. She was a deeply spiritual person. When he first arrived in India, he was all about preaching and tending to the poor and needy. For him, the focus was on ..." she hesitated for a moment before saying, "doing stuff. Then he met Uma and I think he recognized that that wasn't enough."

"He needed to work on himself," observed Sid in a soft voice.

"Exactly. He discovered that inner growth isn't only possible – it's essential, if we *really* wish to help others. After that he disrobed. Built his little cottage. Withdrew from the world."

For a while there was only the sound of the wind blowing down the Kangra Valley, rippling through the trees, and bringing with it the fragrances of a dozen different evening meals in a beguiling spicy fusion.

"This is a paradox, yes?" Ricardo, Heidi's partner, who was sitting next to her, didn't tend to say very much. But when he spoke, it was usually to make a useful point. From the puzzled expression on his face, it was clear that he didn't understand how seclusion from the world could best help others.

Sitting on a bean bag, Ludo who had been silent until now, fixed him with a penetrating look. "A very great paradox," he confirmed. "One that I encountered on my first week in McLeod Ganj and have continued to encounter in many different guises. 'Why don't Buddhists open more soup kitchens?' That's something you hear a lot. 'X, Y and Z religious groups are helping the hungry and needy, what's wrong with you lot?' or 'How can you talk about loving kindness the whole time, but hardly lift a finger to help others?'"

Serena interjected, "Or 'What's the point of retreating to a cave for years, instead of going out into the world and doing something useful?!'"

There were chuckles from some of the other students. Ricardo didn't disguise his perplexity.

"But it's understandable," Sid spoke softly, shooting a sympathetic glance towards Ricardo. "*Bodhichitta* is supposed to be the greatest expression of compassion," said Ricardo. "So why *not* devote one's life to helping other beings through charitable work?"

"The actual definition of *bodhichitta*," Ludo's voice had a calm clarity, "is 'for the sake of others, the wish to attain enlightenment'. Other beings, not only oneself, are the basis of our motivation. When we witness the suffering being endured by those around us, we wish not only to end it," he was looking back again at Ricardo, "but to end it completely. Permanently. The only way that can happen, is for them to realize the true nature of reality – *shunyata* – directly. And the very best way for us to help them do that, is by attaining enlightenment ourselves.

"Even if we were to feed every hungry being in the world – heal everyone, right now, who is sick – the effect of our kindness would be temporary. It wouldn't be long before they were suffering again, because the cause for them to suffer is still present in their mind."

"Karma?" queried Ricardo, who had been living here for long enough to understand the basics.

Ludo nodded. "We suffer because we believe the world exists in a way that is impossible for it to exist. Out there. Separate from us. Having nothing to do with our mind. Because of that, we do and say things that are the cause of future pain, not realizing that we're hurting ourselves. We do this all the time. Others can bring temporary relief, but until we see the truth for ourselves, we will keep experiencing pain and creating the causes for more of it. This ..." Ludo was circling his index finger in the motion of a wheel, "is *samsara*. The cycle of suffering. Birth, ageing, sickness, death. On and on without end.

"How to stop it?" he continued, blue eyes clear in the twilight. "By realizing *shunyata*. How to free others permanently from suffering? By helping them realize it too. Which we best do when we've realized it ourselves. As fully enlightened beings, we have capabilities beyond what any of us currently imagine."

In the softness of that darkening evening, our small group on the balcony felt like a band of passengers traversing an eternal ocean. All too aware of the endless darkness around us, but heading inexorably towards a destination of the most spectacular transcendence, one intimated by the scarlet peaks of the mountains, the crimson rivers flowing from them to a hundred valleys below.

"I like the comparison of the woman who wants to help others through medicine," Sid spoke after a pause. "She can become a First Aid volunteer. After a few days training, she can administer CPR, do wound care, and help people with trauma. All very useful, and she can start right away. Alternatively, if she enrolls as a medical student, it will be seven years before she qualifies. That's a lot of time *not* helping people. But when she graduates, her ability to help others is dramatically greater than the First Aid volunteer."

Ricardo was nodding as he processed this. "We cultivate enlightenment first, so that we can better help others?"

"The three approaches to *bodhichitta*," said Serena, looking up at Ludo expectantly.

He met her glance with a wry smile. "Well, you explain them, my dear. You don't have to rely on me – thank heavens!"

Serena glanced over at Ricardo. "There are said to be three approaches to *bodhichitta,* or the mind of enlighten-ment. Shepherd-like *bodhichitta* is the most altruistic of all motivations – where we place the welfare of others before our own. Only once all other beings are free from *samsara*, will we finally attain enlightenment for ourselves. Boatman-like *bodhichitta* is when we ferry all other beings to safety on the same raft that we're on, arriving at a state of enlightenment together with them. King-like bodhichitta is when we ourselves become enlightened, so that we're in the most powerful position to help others. This," she said, "is the way it is said to happen, although we are encouraged to adopt the shepherd-like approach."

"And if we are yogis," Merrilee couldn't resist, "it may be more like the boatman, when we see ourselves and everything in the world around us as divine."

"Big subject," confirmed Ludo, after a while.

Ricardo, who had been absorbing everything with keen attention, was still looking bemused. "There's one thing, especially, I don't get," he was looking at Ludo. "We all need to understand, to experience *shunyata*, right," he spoke carefully, trying to find the right words, "if we are to become enlightened?"

Ludo nodded.

"And for that, we must practice single-pointed concentration."

"Yes," confirmed Ludo.

"But Sid just said," Ricardo gestured towards him, "that *bodhichitta* is the ultimate manifestation of compassion."

"That's also true," agreed Ludo.

"So how is it that we can focus single-pointedly on *shunyata*, but at the same time be thinking about saving others from unhappiness – *bodhichitta*?"

Ludo, Sid and Serena looked at Ricardo with the highest regard.

"Young man," said Ludo. "*That* is a question it takes most people years of practice to get to. How to practice *bodhichitta* and *shunyata* simultaneously."

Suddenly I was back at Namgyal temple, listening to Geshe Wangpo's teaching on the night that Lorenzo had attended with his splendid notebook and Luna edition pen. How Geshe-la had reached out with his hand, flicking his index and forefingers up and down, talking about how *bodhichitta* and *shunyata* were like the wings of a bird, both necessary to attain enlightenment. How *shunyata* was to be recollected in every act of kindness or compassion. How that would transform the cause of mundane happiness into the transcendent variety that propels us to enlightenment. And how, indeed, the Dalai Lama had told India's Top 10 Social Media Influencers Under 30 about the importance of these two practices.

Now it was Ludo's turn to consider his words carefully. "When we first hear about *bodhichitta*, even the idea that we might want to attain enlightenment to help all other beings is new. Different. It takes time to become familiar with it, let alone to accept it. This form of selflessness and the scale of it is unheard of for most people.

"Then, as we become more accustomed to it, it's no longer just an object of the mind. An idea. It becomes something we really want to embody. We wish to take it on for ourselves. Then it's not so much a state of mind – it also becomes a state of heart. Little by little, we start to see reality through the lens of *bodhichitta*. You might say it's like seeing the world through sunglasses. You have become so familiar with *bodhichitta* that it is now part of how you view things.

"The mind propelled by that state of heart," Ludo continued, "is the mind we train in single-pointed concentration. So, we're not trying to think of two things at once, rather we are subjects, motivated by *bodhichitta*, focusing on the object of *shunyata*."

Ricardo was nodding slowly. "It is a lot to understand."

"Yes."

"I am fortunate that you can explain it to me."

Across the balcony, lit only by the glow of light coming from inside, Ludo told him, "It is my privilege."

"Sometimes," said Serena, "having to explain the *Dharma* out loud helps us clarify our own understanding of it."

"I may have already heard these things from Geshe Wangpo," Ricardo confessed. "But there is always so much to take in."

Franc, who was sitting next to Serena, continued on her theme. "The Buddha, *Dharma* and *Sangha* are sometimes likened to a doctor, the medicine prescribed, and a nurse. We need all three. Other students who have been around the block a few times more than we have – the *Sangha* – they often have a lot to teach us."

"Definitely!" chimed Serena. "Down at the café over the years, I've heard to many things that have helped me understand teachings in ways I never expected."

"Well," Ricardo glanced around gratefully. "Now I can see

how *bodhichitta* and *shunyata* come together. And why that must happen, if we truly wish to help others."

Heidi glanced at his face, squeezing his hand.

"And…" he smiled, "shepherd-like *bodhichitta*."

Darkness had settled completely, and the icy caps of the mountains were now only faint white silhouettes in the distance. Squares of orange had appeared up and down the valley in the windows of countless homes, and the cooling breeze brought with it the fresh scent of Himalayan pine.

It was Flavia, a Spanish woman in her 30s and longstanding yoga student, who spoke now for the first time. "My favorite verse from Shantideva is in his final chapter," she murmured.

Before she said another word, I knew what she was about to say. It was a verse I'd heard His Holiness repeat often. Whether in a Zoom call with hundreds of people, a smaller audience at home, or just the two of us meditating together. The words and the sentiment they expressed were as familiar as they were timelessly transcendent. Flavia quoted, her voice mellifluous in the darkness:

"For as long as space endures,
And for as long as living beings remain,
Until then may I, too, abide,
to dispel the misery of the world."

Uplifted by the exquisite verse, I watched my mind raised from its usual preoccupations to a place of infinite altruism. On that Himalayan balcony, we were inspired to a place beyond self and other, where all beings were in a state of exalted and enduring bliss.

Chapter Nine

I heard him before I saw him. Sprawled, on an overcast morning, across the filing cabinet in the Executive Assistants' office, I heard an explosive baritone guffaw from the stairwell, followed by further reverberations drawing closer. I recognized their source immediately. Without a word being said, a picture appeared in my mind of the man who had only recently arrived in McLeod Ganj. With such a distinctive and magnetic presence, it was as though he had been a prominent member of our little community for years.

One of the security staff was hovering at the door, before Tenzin, looking up, nodded. Moments later, the rotund form was being ushered into the room, unusually attired in suit and tie.

"Blake Ballantyne," he extended his hand first to Tenzin, then to Oliver, as the two men stood.

"I really don't want to disturb you, but I need that signature of consent."

"Ah!" Tenzin glanced at the document in Blake's hand. "The gate camera?"

Blake nodded, his glance drawn to the top of the filing cabinet where I had raised my head. "The ubiquitous cat!" he declaimed with great amusement. "What secrets she must know! Whenever something interesting happens," he gestured extravagantly, "there she is!"

Tenzin and Oliver both turned towards me with wry smiles.

"She does have a certain …" Tenzin was struggling to find the right word.

"Omniscience?" proposed Oliver, blue eyes sparkling behind his glasses.

"I was going to say *savviness*," Tenzin's tone was droll. "About places. And people." Turning back towards his visitor, in that knowing diplomatic way he had of saying things without uttering a word, seeming to imply that the fact Blake Ballantyne had already met me was no coincidence.

Blake occupied a nearby chair to which Tenzin gestured, then both Executive Assistants resumed their seats, while studying the document that their visitor had brought. I recalled how, during the past few weeks, the builders' and painters' trucks which had been such frequent visitors to the old sanatorium across the road had been replaced by those from gardeners, furniture stores and interior décor suppliers. Observing all this from my vantage point on the bench under the cedar tree in the garden next door, I had gathered that The Sanatorium for

Broke Old Bohemians, the vision of my late dear friend, artist Christopher Ackland, was about to become a reality.

Usually, the transformation of a rambling old building so very close to home would have prompted many site inspections by me. What joy was to be found in a golden pyramid of fresh builder's sand! But the driveway of the old sanatorium was very steep, my rear legs wonky, and my energy levels no longer those of a kitten. Instead, I'd had to content myself observing the comings and goings of tradespeople, and the imagined transformation of the rambling double-storied, colonial mansion at the top of the hill.

As Tenzin scanned through the document Blake had handed him, from the remarks they exchanged I gathered that the new rest house was to have security fencing and electric gates fitted, as well as cameras mounted on the replastered posts facing not only the driveway, but also the garden opposite which belonged to Namgyal Monastery. As such, the permission of Namgyal must be granted prior to installation. The monastery had already agreed in principle, but a signature was required. This being a formality, Tenzin had taken out his fountain pen and was executing the document.

Blake clambered to his feet and was readying himself to leave, when there was a flurry of footsteps outside. The Dalai Lama appeared in the doorway.

"Your Holiness," Tenzin spoke, as he and Oliver rose swiftly. "This is Blake Ballantyne, director of the new rest house across the road." He gestured in that direction.

"Good, good!" murmured the Dalai Lama, folding his

hands to his chest in greeting.

Blake reciprocated smoothly, the glow about his features appearing especially seraphic.

"I am pleased that you are here," His Holiness nodded. "I heard about the new residence and I have a request to make."

"Of course, Your Holiness."

As so often with the Dalai Lama, it suddenly seemed as if Blake Ballantyne's appearance was anything but unexpected, the form-filling merely a pretext for a more important assignment – albeit one Blake hadn't known about.

"Please?" His Holiness gestured for Blake to follow him to his rooms.

I would like to have been on my regular windowsill at that moment. Drowsiness, dear reader, held me back – along with the certain knowledge that if anything of piquancy was being discussed, I would be sure to find out about it in the fullness of time. Resting my head back on the top of the cabinet, I resumed my gentle slumbers until disturbed some minutes later by an eruption of laughter, the Dalai Lama's chuckling coalescing with that of Blake Ballantyne. The two men had emerged after a brief meeting and were pausing in the doorway looking directly at me.

"Quite extraordinary!" Blake was shaking his head, jovially. *"Bangalore Crushes Rajasthan by Nine Wickets."*

The reference to this specific sports headline may mean nothing to most people but was of the utmost personal relevance to me. It was one that I hadn't heard mentioned for many years. Why was it resurfacing right now?

Blake continued gazing at me. "She must be the luckiest cat alive!" he declared.

"Yes," the Dalai Lama was smiling. "And perhaps we are the luckiest of people!"

THE DAY DOZED GENTLY BY, LOW GREY CLOUDS GRADUALLY clearing to give way to the most unexpected of afternoons – pristine and glorious, the air pine-crisp with promise. I decided to visit the garden next door, Blake Ballantyne's visit having made me curious to check on any changes to the old sanatorium gateway. Plus, for another reason, the garden had recently taken on a poignant significance.

On several occasions since that evening of their first encounter, Binita and Lorenzo had returned to sit under the cedar tree. Binita was conservative and restrained by nature; despite her evident attraction to Lorenzo, she was not the kind of woman who would invite a man to the home she shared with her daughters. For his part Lorenzo, courtly to a fault, wasn't about to jeopardize the extraordinary, even metaphysical, connection he sensed linked him to Binita.

Which made the garden the perfect place to spend time together – a public space, yet in reality quite private. An arboreal retreat with mountain views where they could talk for hours in the way that new-found lovers do, thrilling in the joy of exploration, discovering mutual fervors and fascinations, lost in each other from the rest of the world.

On that particular afternoon it wasn't long after I had

found my way to the garden, doing the rounds of the shrubs in the hope of discovering a new cutting of catnip, when I heard their voices. Arriving in the garden, they were soon sitting on the bench. And from their rising excitement, I could tell that a fresh discovery had been made.

"How did they find it?" Binita asked Lorenzo, staring into his eyes.

"They were cleaning around the plaque. You know, the one you found? There was more space to the right of Nonno's coffin, so they were digging there. Just a small excavation. Enough for the urn with Nonna's ashes to be placed. To begin with, the workmen thought it was just a piece of bark. Something jammed on the side of the coffin." He was opening a folder and showing her the contents.

"A message?" queried Binita.

"From a friend, I'm guessing," Lorenzo was looking down.

The two of them were so engrossed they hardly noticed me approach, hopping onto the bench beside them and scrutinizing the object of their preoccupation. It was an ancient and mud-smeared flap of black leather, perhaps once rectangular in shape but now scarred and asymmetric. The edges were worn and ragged with age. Reaching with forefinger and thumb, it took Lorenzo some moments to get a cautious grip of the leather, sliding his hand beneath and turning it over with the utmost care, to keep it from disintegrating into a hundred pieces.

The leather flap enclosed a single sheet of decaying sepia-colored paper. The handwritten message it contained was so faded and stained it was almost unreadable. Only a few words stood out.

"*Lorenzo*," Binita read them out. "*Wheat.*" Then after a long pause, "Does that say *ground*?"

Lorenzo was nodding. "I think so. It's so faint ..."

A black mark completely obscured whatever came next. Before they both read in unison, "*Many seeds.*"

They were silent for a long while.

"A mystery," Lorenzo stared down.

Drawing it closer to her face, Binita inspected the page with sharp acuity. "Is that a name at the bottom?" she asked. "Lorenzo is at the top. At the end could it be ... John?"

Lorenzo followed her fingertip with an uncertain expression. "A friend perhaps?"

"Someone who visited later? After Padre was buried?"

"If only I'd come years ago, when Nonna was still alive." Lorenzo turned towards her, his face only inches from hers.

"If you had," she told him quickly, "you wouldn't have met me."

"In that case," he said as they laughed, "I'm glad I didn't come years ago. All the same, this message is a mystery on top of all the other mysteries."

Binita gazed at him adoringly.

"And I still don't know what to put on the headstone, but I need to tell the engravers before the end of today."

He looked away to the distant mountains before musing. "Nothing happens for years and years, then suddenly *everything* happens at once – and destiny is decided in a few short days."

At that moment, Blake Ballantyne's old Jaguar pulled into the driveway opposite and made its throaty way up the short hill. In the back was the silhouette of two shaven heads.

As they watched the vehicle retreat from view, Binita sat more upright. "About the headstone, do you know the sentiments you wish to express?" she queried.

Lorenzo nodded.

"But you need to find the words," she confirmed.

"Or a quotation. Something to honor both Nonno and Nonna. What they held to be important."

Binita turned to him with an expression of sudden brightness. "I think I know who can help."

Moments later she was standing. Lorenzo followed suit. As they started away from the bench I meowed plaintively.

"Oh, HHC. We have been ignoring you!" Binita turned.

"The holy cat!" Lorenzo reached over to stroke my head. "She has been sitting with us all this time."

"I think she should come with us," said Binita in a tone of voice I recognized. One that Lorenzo evidently recognized too, because moments later he had handed her the folder and lifted me. As they stepped across the garden, then the street, before making their way up the driveway of the new rest house, he had me in his arms. My whiskers tingled with the citrus tones of his Italian aftershave, the scent of those faraway Mediterranean vistas which seemed to cling to him wherever he went.

All too soon we were arriving at the top of the driveway, where the rest house building was a resplendent and magnificent vision in white. Workmen in overalls were busy on the veranda and in the garden. Floating ahead of us in a lilac sari, Binita was inquiring about Blake Ballantyne, before being shown down a corridor covered in painting sheets, the smell of fresh water-based paint combining with the scents of floor wax and brass polish in a profusion of giddying newness.

"Binita!" An explosion echoed from a chamber to the left of the corridor.

At the far side of a capacious reception room, Blake Ballantyne was in conversation with two monks, who were responding to him with great deference. Leaving them to some unknown task, Blake was soon approaching her. "To what do I owe the pleasure?"

"I can see you are very busy," Binita wasted no time. "But we have a request."

"Come through," he waved us further down the passage. "Good heavens!" he exclaimed, when he saw Lorenzo holding me. "The Dalai Lama's Cat! Twice in one day!"

"She's been here already?" asked Lorenzo.

"I was there," replied Blake. "This is an inaugural visit for all three of you."

IN MINUTES WE WERE SHOWN INTO HIS OFFICE – A ROOM, DEAR reader, like no other. A huge grand chamber with soaring ceilings, opposite us was a wide bay window looking across terraced lawns to the majestic Himalayas. Set into the wall on the left was a baronial fireplace, its mantelpiece as high as a person's shoulders. To the right, the gleaming sweep of a mahogany desk. As Lorenzo stepped inside, Blake gestured towards a sofa and two wingback chairs that were ranged about a coffee table. "Please do sit," he invited. Then as Lorenzo shot him an inquiring glance, he nodded.

Moments later, I was placed on the new carpet like the most fragile of writing instruments. I was free to roam! It was the décor, rather than the lofty scale of the room that was of interest to a cat. And Blake Ballantyne's new refuge was filled with objects I'd never seen before, and aromas I had never smelled – in short, dear reader, a veritable treasure trove.

"Your room is astonishing!" It was Binita who first voiced the response that all three of us visitors evidently felt.

"Truly amazing!" echoed Lorenzo.

On either side of the fireplace, bookcases rose floor to ceiling, the shiny black paint fresh and pungent, although quite dry. I got up on my haunches and peered into one of the lower shelves, before launching myself onto it. The contents were not those of ordinary shelves. Not only were the books more ancient, redolent of faraway places and distant times, but interspersed with them were the most unexpected discoveries. A large, highly polished malachite box with brass corners, replete with egg-size semiprecious stones of tiger's eye, amethyst and rose quartz. Further along, some unknown instrument fashioned from dark wood, a variety of hammered metal keys curving upwards. I sniffed at it tentatively.

"My bric-a-brac." Blake was modest. "I shipped the whole lot with me when I came from California."

"Really," Lorenzo sounded interested. "Which part?"

"San Anselmo," Blake replied. "Marin County. The American Mediterranean – at least, that's how I like to think of it. The same feel as the Alpine foothills, but instead of Como, they overlook the Bay of San Francisco. The closest thing you can find to the Italian Riviera."

"As an Italian," Lorenzo met his eyes chuckling gleefully, "I have to say this is true! I always liked that part of San Francisco and now you have explained why!"

I continued my explorations as the humans sat, but I had already recognized that this chamber, with its many curiosities, would take a great many visits to become acquainted with. Not least of which, ranged on the wall behind where Lorenzo and Binita were sitting, were row upon row of the most astonishing African and Native American tribal masks.

Hopping off the shelf and walking to the bay window, my attention was captured by a large urn-like object, resting on a table near a banquette that followed the curve of the window. Once on the banquette, I reached out with my paw to this most exceptional item, one that seemed conjured from an era so ancient it was beyond imagining and made from a substance I had never encountered.

"With unerring instinct, His Holiness's Cat finds her way to the most hallowed object in the room," I heard Blake's voice rumbling in the distance. "And one with perhaps the most direct association to herself."

I glanced up to find all three humans watching me.

"An Indian antique?" queried Binita.

Lorenzo was studying it closely. "Or maybe Greek?" he

hazarded.

After a pause, Blake replied, "I'll give you fifty per cent each. It's from Gandhara, the Indo-Greek kingdom that existed more than two thousand years ago."

As his two guests gazed awe-struck, he continued, "You know Gandhara, the origin of the Buddha statue? Shakyamuni never wanted a statue of himself to be made. But when the Greeks invaded India about three hundred years after his time, and some began to follow his teachings, they couldn't help themselves. They were so used to immortalizing Hellenistic gods that they wanted to do the same thing for this man-god they revered. And so they gave us the classical Buddha with his Mediterranean curly hair and topknot. An image of enlightenment that became increasingly Asiatic the further east it travelled."

"Quite extraordinary!" Lorenzo was shaking his head.

"That stone casket once contained relics of the Buddha – at least, according to the inscription."

"It must be very old," said Binita.

"About two thousand years," Blake told them.

Binita moaned softly.

Binita and Lorenzo sat together on the sofa, as Blake faced them. Glancing over, he noticed the folder they had brought with them, which had fallen open.

"Something quite ancient there too, by the look of things," he observed.

"A very recent discovery," said Lorenzo, before telling him the story of his grandfather. From the way Blake sat in his chair listening with rapt attention, it was evident that the tale of Padre Lorenzo's voyage to India full of religious conviction, his intense challenges of faith, and subsequent discovery of a much broader perspective was one that was both engaging yet somehow familiar. When Lorenzo told him about Uma and the fire, and how half a century of dislocation had, only in the past few days, been almost magically resolved, Blake's eyes were bright with possibility.

"Let me see that," he said, when Lorenzo had finished explaining the discovery of the page next to Nonno's grave.

"It's almost impossible to read," Binita told him.

"I like a good mystery," he replied, taking the folder and adjusting his glasses.

As Lorenzo and Binita watched from the sofa, I settled on the bay window banquette. With comfortable cushions upholstered in a soft tartan fabric, I decided that, henceforth, *my* place in Blake Ballantyne's inner sanctum was to be here beside the Gandharan casket. Decision made, I set about a vigorous grooming session, making sure to cast off several distinctive tufts of fine white fur to make this place my own.

Like Binita and Lorenzo, Blake picked out the same words as he stared at the page, concentrating fiercely.

"It seems to be a message left by someone called John," said Binita. "I think that's the name at the bottom."

Blake held the folder closer as he stared at it, before exhaling loudly. "Ah yes!" he said, placing it back on the table. "A message from John, indeed."

From the gleam in his eye, it was clear that he knew more.

Both Binita and Lorenzo were staring at him.

"Saint John, unless I am mistaken. A verse from that most spiritual of the gospels: *Very truly I tell you, unless a kernel of wheat falls to the ground and dies, it remains only a single seed. But if it dies, it produces many seeds.*"

Lorenzo had seized the folder and was nodding. "Yes!" his voice rose in excitement. He was handing it to Binita. "But I wonder why that verse?"

"Perhaps it was a favorite of the Padre's," suggested Blake. "Or perhaps that's how others saw him."

"But what does it mean?" Binita looked up from the folder.

Blake sat back in his chair. "If a seed thinks of itself as only a seed, as a small, shiny object destined always to stay that way, it will never fulfil its true purpose," he explained. "For that to happen, the seed must face complete destruction. Its shell must crack. Everything it knows itself to be must change. The real purpose of the seed looks nothing like a seed – it is a plant that in time, like it says, will produce many more seeds."

"It's a verse," Binita's eyes shone luminously. "Like the one we spoke of before – at the café?"

"From the *Chandogya Upanishad*?" Blake confirmed. "Yes. A verse of transformation, you might say. One that recognizes that the seat of consciousness," he brought a hand to his heart, "this lotus shrine, holds possibilities far beyond what our very limited physical form may suggest. Like the seed, our potential is as different and as great as this vast universe."

"This idea is in Christianity too?" Lorenzo was surprised.

'Oh yes," nodded Blake. "It is the same wisdom known

by many different names – *moksha*, *bodhi*, *kaivalya* or *satori* in Asian spiritual traditions. The idea of identifying with a boundless and quite blissful state, wide as the universe, which transcends individual personality. These ideas were understood long before Jesus was born. They would have been well known to someone as spiritually inquiring as him."

"I didn't realize that Jesus taught transcendence," said Lorenzo.

"In my opinion," Blake nodded pointedly, "it is one of the great tragedies that Christianity evolved in such a way that it became caught up with morality and guilt, so it lacks much interest in self-knowledge, beyond the merely psychological. Most people are unaware of Jesus's profoundest teachings."

"Most people?" queried Lorenzo. "Including Padre Lorenzo?"

Blake glanced down pensively before nodding. "It probably came too late for him," he said after a while, before meeting their scrutiny once again. "The discovery of the Nag Hammadi scrolls."

From the expressions on Binita and Lorenzo's faces, it was clear they had no idea what he was talking about.

"The scrolls were discovered quite by chance in 1945, when an Arab peasant discovered a large earthenware jar containing copies of texts that were in circulation at the beginning of the Christian era. After Jesus's death, his followers were fragmented into groups with quite different ideas about his main teachings. Even the big differences we see between Christian groups today are as nothing compared to those first two hundred years."

Lorenzo and Binita followed him intently.

"I sometimes wonder," Blake looked pensive, "whether, like Buddha, Jesus was perhaps someone who taught people according to their different levels of understanding, their propensities, and so on. A more nuanced, multi-layered approach than we are used to hearing."

"So, God wasn't British after all?" Binita flashed a mischievous glance, reminding him of the idea he had expounded down at The Himalaya Book Café.

Blake roared with laughter. "Good heavens, no! God was … well, Jesus was, if anything quite Buddhist! It's hard to come away from the gnostic texts without recognizing the similarities. They actually suggest that dogmas such as the virgin birth were naive misunderstandings right from the start. The actual point was not that Mary didn't get pregnant in the usual way, but that Jesus chose to be born to benefit others, instead of being propelled into life by karma, like everyone else."

"He was a *bodhisattva!*" exclaimed Lorenzo.

"Exactly," nodded Blake. "I've even heard some claim," Blake's eyes twinkled, "that the wise men recorded as coming from the East were Buddhist lamas coming to discover where their enlightened master had been reborn, as was the custom." He shrugged. "Whatever the truth of that, it seems to me that many of Jesus's most profound teachings have been marginalized or misunderstood. Time and again he spoke of 'the Kingdom of Heaven', which has become dumbed down to some kind of Buckingham Palace tea party," he flashed a grin at Binita, "where only the saved go when they die. But what if the

Kingdom of Heaven is a transcendent state of consciousness?

"*In my Father's house are many places,*" he pointed a finger at Lorenzo's folder. "That's another verse from your John. Many places? He isn't talking about housing projects, but states of consciousness, just as other spiritual traditions describe realms of being more subtle than this one," he nodded thoughtfully. "We access these only after we have let go of what keeps us bound to this dimension of reality: our overweening sense of self. *Whoever desires to save his life will lose it. But whoever loses his life, for my sake, will find it.* What is that, if not a warning about the danger of self-cherishing? The critical importance of letting go of what Buddhists term 'self-grasping ignorance', if we are to experience its opposite: a state of divinity?"

On the couch facing him, Binita and Lorenzo were following with expressions of wonder.

"Why have we not heard of this before?" asked Binita.

"This is not an idea of Christianity I ever knew about," agreed Lorenzo.

Blake shrugged. "There are contemporary sources, like Elaine Pagels, Bart Ehrman and the wonderful Franciscan monk, Richard Rohr. And practitioners stretching all the way back through time. The teachings of the 'wisdom Jesus', whose purpose was to awaken us to our divine energy, require no less contemplation and effort than those of a practicing Buddhist. This is a pathway you must tread for yourself. It is up to you to spend time awakening to the divine within. But understandably, this idea of his teachings turned out to be much less popular than the version which presents Jesus as a divine being we can't possibly imitate, but who, through the offices of the church, will save us. All we must do is believe, and salvation is ours.

"Since the very early days there were tensions," he sighed, "between the groups which became the orthodox church and the rest. As the proto-orthodox church gained power, it tried to destroy the idea that salvation was something you could attain on your own – you had to do it through them. The real game changer came after Roman Emperor Constantine's conversion. Christianity became an officially approved religion in the fourth century. From then on, any scriptures with gnostic elements were termed 'heretical' and destroyed. Mere possession of them became a criminal offence. It's quite likely that, at that time, some heartbroken gnostic monks from the monastery of St. Pachomius hid a trove of their much-loved but banned books in an earthenware jar. Which is where they stayed for the next one and a half millennia."

There was a knocking at the door, before an Indian man appeared. "The monks have nearly finished," he told Blake.

"I'll be ten minutes," he responded.

As he looked back towards his guests, Lorenzo told him, "I only wish my grandfather had known about this."

Blake pondered for a time before saying, "What matters is that he found a path."

Lorenzo gazed at Binita. The two of them were sitting as close as possible without actually touching. In response to a flicker in Binita's eyes, Lorenzo asked, "We actually came to request your advice. Specifically, what to have engraved on the headstone that will mark the graves of Nonno and Nonna."

"The gravestone that Nonna placed there," said Binita. "Read simply: *Here lies the other half of my soul.*"

Blake glanced towards the bookshelves, pensively.

"We are looking for something about them both," said Lorenzo. "A quote, perhaps a phrase that relates to what was important to them."

"Their inner journey," said Binita. "Like that one from the *Upanishads.*"

"Your grandfather," queried Blake. "Became a practicing Buddhist?"

Lorenzo nodded.

"And grandmother?"

"I think also," he said. Then smiling wryly, "But she often used to say that labels didn't matter. You had to go beyond them."

As he spoke the words, a flash of inspiration so animated Blake than he leapt to his feet. "That's it!" he called out in excitement. "She as much as gave you the epitaph herself! Go beyond!"

I had no idea what he meant, dear reader. Nor, it was clear, did Lorenzo or Binita – until he went on to explain. And as soon as he did, the solution he offered was so perfectly coherent, so magnificently appropriate, that the eyes of his visitors were soon shining with the same radiant impulse that burned in his own.

A short while later, his visitors stood to leave. Conversation moved to the interring of Nonna's ashes. How Lorenzo planned to do this in two morning's time – just himself, Sid, Serena, Mrs. Trinci and Binita. It would be a private ceremony, as was appropriate in the circumstances. But afterwards, Lorenzo explained, there were a few people in the local community he wanted to thank. People whose help had been important in different kinds of ways. Sam, the bookstore manager, for example, and of course, Franc and several others from the book café. Binita's colleague Heidi and her uncle Ludo. And Blake himself.

"I know that Mrs. Trinci ..." he began.

"We're not to burden Mrs. Trinci with this," Binita firmly closed any such suggestion. "She already has far too much stress as it is."

"In two days, you said?" Rising to his feet, Blake strolled to the desk near where I was sitting and consulted the calendar on his screen. After a pause he told them, "I have a suggestion."

Lorenzo and Binita were on their way to the door, when Binita turned, looking at me.

"We have left someone behind," she observed.

"The holy cat," said Lorenzo.

All three humans were looking at where I was resting on the tartan cushions of the bay window, next to the Gandhara stone casket.

"Holy cat!" Blake chuckled, touching Lorenzo's shoulder. "So Italian of you!"

"His Holiness's Cat," Lorenzo corrected himself.

Blake was smiling as he looked at me. "Holy comes from the word 'healing' or 'to make whole'. I think she has a very healing presence, so 'holy cat' is a good name for her."

"She looks very settled there," commented Binita.

"She is," said Blake. "Instinct probably guided her to her chosen spot. When she wants to leave, she'll be taken home. I am making particular plans for this."

After the three of them left the room I fell into a gentle doze, lulled by the soft warmth of the cushions, and the sounds of workmen bustling in the chambers and garden around me.

WHEN I BLINKED MY EYES OPEN AGAIN, I SAW THAT BLAKE had returned to the office, sitting in the same chair he'd occupied with Lorenzo and Binita. Facing him were two monks – teenagers by the look of their youthful faces. I gathered that they would be helping settle in the many residents who were to arrive, volunteering their time in exchange for the chance to practice their English. Both, it seemed, were destined for universities overseas.

At first, I didn't think anything of the meeting. Being surrounded by monks in all shapes and sizes on a daily basis, there was nothing unusual about seeing two in conversation with Blake. Then I remembered Blake's visit to the Executive Assistants' office that morning, and how the Dalai Lama had drawn him aside to make a request. How he and His Holiness had returned a short while later, and Blake's outburst about a cricket headline from a newspaper many years ago, that had particular associations for me.

Suddenly wide awake, I studied the silhouette of the

monks intently. Wondering if their presence here and now was connected to the Dalai Lama's request. They were strangers to me. And yet … could it be that, after the passage of more years than I cared to remember, these were grown-up versions of the two novice monks, Sashi and Tashi? Novices who, in turn, had once been the same pair of street urchins who had sold my two kitten siblings, on the streets of Delhi? Who had wrapped me, the unsaleable runt of the litter, in the sports page of *The Times of India* and were about to throw me in the garbage when His Holiness, stuck in a traffic jam and looking on with shock, came to the rescue?

The last I had heard of Sashi and Tashi had been when they were novices, recognizably the same young rascals who had been quite willing to discard me as trash. They would have grown up in the ten years or so since. Could it be that some quirk of karma had returned them to my presence, only this time I was lying on a tartan cushion next to a priceless Buddhist artefact?

Having discussed the many ways in which the monks were to help the sanatorium's new residents, there was a lull in conversation before Blake cleared his throat.

"I have once last … instruction," he said, his tone noticeably stricter than it had previously been.

The two monks, obedient and responsive throughout, adopted the most dutiful expressions.

"I have one visitor, not a resident, who has trouble with her legs. She finds it hard to walk up and down our very steep driveway."

The monks' faces were full of sympathy.

"I haven't known her for long, but she already has a very special place in my heart. And also in the heart of the Dalai Lama, and many other people here in McLeod Ganj."

The monks nodded respectfully.

"She may come to visit at any time of the day, and when she does, it is your job to bring her up the driveway and to take her back down again when she leaves."

"She is in a wheelchair?" asked one of the monks.

Blake shook his head. "You are to carry her."

The two exchanged a glance.

"You won't be breaking your vows!" Blake's voice boomed authoritatively, before leaning towards them. "It's most important that you watch the gate camera screen. Our visitor can't press the buzzer. It's up to you to monitor the driveway, to see when she's there. If she looks like she wants to come inside, you are to collect her."

The monks continued nodding, but from their mystified expressions it was clear that they were apprehensive about this mysterious female caller.

"Do you understand?" queried Blake.

"Yes sir," they chanted in unison.

"Any questions?"

It took a few seconds before one of the monks plucked up the courage. "This visitor. How do we know who she is? Is there a photo?"

"Unnecessary," Blake continued with his stern delivery. "She is sitting right there." And he pointed towards me.

In an instant, the monks were pressing their palms together at their foreheads and bowing reverentially in my direction.

"The Dalai Lama's Cat!" exclaimed one.

Blake nodded. "His Holiness tells me that you know her."

"We do!" said the other monk in an anguished tone. "We can never make up for the harm we caused her."

"Oh, I think you can," countered Blake confidently. "She likes to visit. And I want her to feel welcome. There will be ample opportunity for you to show her all the devotion to be accorded to the true bodhicatva that she is."

His tone was as gruff as the faces of the monks were contrite. Stretching out luxuriantly with a quiver of the front paws, I fixed them with my inscrutable sapphire-blue gaze. I knew the director of the rest house quite well enough to recognize the irrepressible glint of mischief in his eyes.

Chapter Ten

The most exquisite of days are often those that spring upon us unexpectedly. Calendar events, landmark festivities and annual high jinks that have been months in the planning may very well be jolly and bright. But it's spontaneous celebrations, catching us by surprise, that frequently fill us most with joy. Those unplanned encounters and wholly unforeseen reunions that truly make our hearts sing – do they not, dear reader?

That most special of days began for me with nothing more remarkable than a quiet walk. I made my way along the road to where Lorenzo was to inter the remains of his beloved Nonna, next to the rediscovered grave of his Nonno. It was to be a private occasion. Just Lorenzo and those who had been of most immediate help in helping him make this reconnection: Binita, Mrs. Trinci, Serena and Sid. And, of course, me.

I caught the waft of brewing coffee on the driveway to Mrs. Trinci's cottage, along with the smell of fresh baking. The garden was wet with dew and the five humans were standing outside, speaking in low voices, when I arrived. I sniffed the flower beds, always so much more pungent first thing in the morning. I investigated some freshly planted shrubs, savoring the floral bouquets and loamy undertones. My presence, it seemed, was entirely expected. And not long after I had arrived the group was forming a small procession, following the narrow footpath down the side of the garden into the forest. Given the unsteadiness of my gait, I brought up the rear, Sid glancing behind from time to time to check on me.

The gravesite, exactly as Serena had described, wasn't far from the cottage, where the path descended the mountain. It was set in a wall of earth to the left, which was usually shrouded in creeper. Today it was exposed, the creeper trimmed back to reveal a panel of soil in which a neat square hole had been dug, tunnelling some way in, presumably alongside Padre Lorenzo's coffin.

There was a pristine tranquility to the forest that morning. Sunlight streamed through gaps in the branches of the protective umbrella pine high above, forming shafts of light, weightless and ethereal, amid the variegated greenery. Around us the undergrowth was dense and herbaceous, dominated by thickets of rhododendrons, flowering in pink and crimson profusion. From time to time a bird would dive from the branches, leaving behind a swoop of mellifluous song, which dissipated back into the soft quietude of the morning.

Burlap sacks had been laid on the path, and there was a wheelbarrow containing builder's sand and a shiny new trowel. Holding a small urn-shaped casket in both hands, its porcelain surface decorated with a lotus flower motif, Lorenzo turned to Binita, who was standing beside him, followed my Mrs. Trinci, Serena and Sid. I watched from a short distance behind Sid, a bend in the path giving me a clear view.

"This still feels somehow extraordinary to me." Lorenzo's voice was soft as the morning breeze, murmuring through the trees. "When I first arrived in India, I hoped that finding Nonno's grave may be possible. In a cemetery perhaps. Some official place. I never dreamed of it happening this way. Making such personal connections to you who have been so kind," he was meeting each of them in the eye. "Also, discovering this sacred place."

A Himalayan bulbul appeared from nowhere, perching unusually close to Lorenzo on a nearby branch, twitching its mohawk crest as it turned its head this way and that, seeming to focus on the casket in his hands. Before flying away.

"I am sorry that my dear Pappa wasn't able to do this for you Nonna," Lorenzo nodded towards the casket. "Perhaps it is karma. But I don't think Pappa ever felt the connection to this place that I did. Even when I was a little boy, the stories you told me made me want to come. And now that I am here," he gazed at Binita, "I feel like I belong."

Binita returned his expression, eyes gleaming.

"Back then, when I was still young, Nonna showed me how to meditate. I can still see us sitting on the balcony at our place in Ravello under the umbrella pines, looking towards the Mediterranean. She taught me how to sit with a straight back. To focus on breathing. She also taught me a mantra, so long ago I thought that I'd lost it forever.

"In spring and summer, when the Mediterranean sky was clear, we could see far into the distance, along the coastline to the towns and beaches. The ships in the sea, leaving trails of white waves on the dark blue surface. It felt like we were Gods looking down on creation. But then when winter came, there were only clouds, mist and rain for weeks. We were freezing cold, and there was no visibility. We could see nothing at all. All the beauty of the summer felt like only a dream. A vision without substance.

"Nonna used to tease me. She used to say, 'What sea do you mean, Renzo' – that was her name for me. 'What ships? *How* do they exist?'" Lorenzo paused, gazing at the others. "I was too young to know it then, but I realize now what she was doing. Even at that young age, she was starting to train me in the Buddhist idea of *shunyata*. That all we perceive may not be as solid as we believe it to be. Illusion-like."

Sid and Serena were nodding.

"So many things have come to make sense to me, even in these past few days. You know, for a long time I had wondered that if this moment was ever to come, if I had the chance to place Nonna's remains next to Nonno's, what marker should I leave for the two of them, side by side. Should I choose something from the Buddha *Dharma*? From the *Upanishads*? The *Bible*?

"Binita and I went to see Signor Ballantyne at the rest house. I explained my dilemma. We were discussing many things and I mentioned how Nonna used to say we need to go beyond labels. That was when he shared a mantra with us." A sudden charge of electricity came into his eyes. "It turned out to be the same mantra I used to recite with Nonna all those years ago, but I had forgotten! The one she once taught me!"

The others were smiling.

"As a child, imitating Nonna, I didn't understand what the words meant or where they came from. That she was teaching me the mantra from *The Heart Sutra*: *Go beyond, go completely beyond*. Signor Ballantyne says that the mantra is among the most powerful formulas for understanding *shunyata* to be found. That in just a few words it sets out how to attain the perfection of wisdom and, ultimately, complete enlightenment."

Serena and Sid were smiling in agreement.

"Then Sid," Lorenzo nodded towards him, "made his own marvelous suggestion."

Sid lifted a black folder he was holding in his right hand. "That we recite *The Heart Sutra*," he said.

"I can think of nothing more fitting, not only for Nonna, but for Nonno too."

Sid opened the folder and handed out a single page to Mrs. Trinci, Serena and Binita. "Sutras," he murmured, "are the spoken words of Shakyamuni Buddha and his most enlightened followers. And *The Heart Sutra* is the shortest teaching on the essence of the Perfection of Wisdom, the Blessed Mother."

"The Blessed Mother!" Mrs. Trinci repeated fervently.

"Wisdom, *shunyata*, is sometimes called that," explained Sid, a twinkle about his lips. "Because the mother is the one who gives birth to everything. All arises from the divine feminine."

They began, in unison, reading the text of *The Heart Sutra*, Binita holding a sheet for Lorenzo and her to share. They were words I'd heard recited a thousand times or more, about how Buddha was staying in Rajgir, at Vulture Peak, and how in his presence, his student, the venerable Shariputra, asks the *bodhisattva* Avalokiteshvara how *Dharma* students should train in the perfection of wisdom. Avalokiteshvara explains that they should see all things as being empty of inherent existence. Not only all things, but also all attainments. After which he recites the mantra of the perfection of wisdom: *tadyatha om gaté gaté paragaté parasamgaté bodhi svaha*

And as they recited the mantra, Lorenzo turned to place the small casket of his Nonna's remains in the earth wall next to those of his Nonno, pushing it firmly to the back of the cavity. Then he lifted a trowel of sand and tipped it into the space, before filling it in with several more loads.

"Om gaté gaté paragaté parasamgaté bodhi svaha," they all repeated. And when they did, it felt less like a somber interment than an uplifting commemoration of the love and wisdom that Padre Lorenzo and Uma had shared. Not the closing of a loop so much as the widening of a spiral, that had begun with just the two of them all those years ago and had spun outwards through the whorl of time, to include not only Lorenzo and their other direct descendants, but all those who had been

touched by their lives and story. The small group gathered here and now. Others in Italy, India and who knew where else?

For what was the wisdom of *shunyata* if it didn't include an understanding of dependency and interconnectedness? Under the canopy that morning, with the diffused light filtering through the trees and forest birds diving and looping, seldom was there such a tangible evocation of the ceaseless ebb and flow of karmic currents that propelled living beings and all that they could perceive through limitless time and space.

The short ceremony ended with a recitation of the four immeasurables:

> *May all beings have happiness and the true causes of happiness.*
> *May all beings be free from suffering and the true causes of suffering.*
> *May all beings never be parted from the happiness that is beyond suffering – great nirvana liberation.*
> *May all beings abide in peace and equanimity, their minds free from attachment, aversion and free from ignorance.*

AFTERWARDS, WE RETURNED FROM THE FOREST FOLLOWING the same single file in which we'd set out. There were only the soft morning sounds of the forest. The babble of a nearby stream carried by a mountain breeze through branches. The gentle drone of bees in the rhododendron blossoms.

In that sylvan place there was a sense of resolution, now that the remains of Nonno and Nonna had been placed together. And of peace, the original purpose of Lorenzo's mission having been fulfilled.

Our small procession continued up the side of Mrs. Trinci's property, where we were joined by Rishi, who had been playing inside with his nanny. Emerging from the forest, the morning was brilliant with light. And as we headed towards Tara Crescent, a figure appeared in the distance from the direction of Sid and Serena's home. Tall and slender, in the dazzling brightness I didn't recognize her immediately, but she was moving in a way that was nimbly familiar.

Serena, Sid and Rishi paused for a moment. The pace of the approaching young woman was increasing as she drew closer. In front, Lorenzo and Mrs. Trinci were waiting too. Perhaps it was my failing eyesight. Maybe also the fact that I hadn't seen her for three years; in the time she'd been at university overseas, she had grown from a girl into a mature young woman. It was only moments before she came directly towards me and threw herself on the ground that I recognized her – Zahra!

Zahra was Sid's daughter from his first marriage, and she and I shared a powerful bond. The little girl whose mother had died in a tragic car accident not long before I was born. Through Yogi Tarchin, we had both come to understand the reason why we felt the most extraordinary close connection.

"My darling!" she was on the grass, stroking me effusively.

I chirruped softly, butting her forehead and rubbing her face with mine.

"I got home last night! I'm so happy to see you!"

As was I, dear reader! There were no words for my joy at this entirely unexpected reunion. I found that I was purring loudly.

"Oh, little HHC!" She was standing again, scooping me in her arms up to her shoulder, as she had since she was a little girl. Now I was above the eye level of the others, except for Sid. All looking at us with the most endearing expressions.

"The Most Beautiful Creature That Ever Lived," said Mrs. Trinci. "That is what I have always called her." She paused reflectively, reaching out to Zahra. "Now, I think, perhaps there are two of you!"

We continued out the driveway and into Tara Crescent, turning right towards McLeod Ganj.

"I've so missed you HHC!" Zahra murmured, as we followed the others. "I have you on my screensaver. You're often in my thoughts. I hope you know that."

There had been no conscious awareness of such a thing. But I had always sensed that, while far distant, our heart connection remained – loving, poignant, abiding. Now that she was so dramatically here and now, as she carried me, I relished the reconnection. Savoring the uniquely familiar sensation of her touch. The delicate glow of her flawless skin. Inhaling her in the here and now.

I paid little attention to where we were going until we had already turned up the steep short drive leading to the rest house and were nearing the summit. Making our way along the newly paved path to what was now the grand entrance, large tubs of scarlet geraniums flanking the great arched wooden doors on either side of a large reception room.

This, evidently, had been Blake Ballantyne's suggestion, when Lorenzo and Binita had consulted with him earlier that week. Lorenzo had wanted to thank some of those in the wider community who had been such a support to him, after the private interment. Blake had evidently invited him to do this at the rest house.

The old building, until so recently dilapidated, had been restored to a most serene glory. It wasn't an especially large building, but it had a stately presence perched atop a hill, its gabled roof featuring ornate wooden panels decorated in intricate Indian designs. Both the ground floor living areas and upstairs bedrooms led onto verandas that wrapped around the whole building, their gleaming white balustrades complementing the freshly painted sandstone-colored walls. Sheer curtains gusted through the open doors leading onto the balconies, upstairs and down. Through the billowing folds of fabric were glimpses of the rooms within; it was a mansion ripe for exploration!

Trailing the others, Zahra carried me to the cool shade of the broad veranda and swept between the curtains of one of the arched French doorways. In the large reception room, some very familiar people were gathering. Franc, Sam and Bronnie with their baby had just arrived from The Himalaya Book Café and were being served coffee and cool drinks by staff, circulating with trays.

Ludwig and a few of the long-term students from The Downward Dog School of Yoga were clustered around Marianne Ponter, from the nearby nursing home. Marianne was gesturing towards a painting by Christopher Ackland, her late former resident, whose entirely unexpected posthumous success had made the rebirth of the rest house possible. Ricardo and Heidi had settled onto one of the many large and inviting sofas, scattered with plush velvet cushions in an assortment of colors – deep green, cobalt and magenta.

I wriggled to be put down. Zahra obliged as Sid and Serena paused to introduce her to Blake Ballantyne, resplendent in a dark jacket and cravat, who was welcoming everyone as they arrived. Glancing at his watch, he seemed eager to get started on things. For my own part, I couldn't wait to investigate this wondrous new room with all its decorative *objets*, from blue and white ceramic temple jars ranged on side tables to intriguing sticks of perfume diffuser, wafting exotic fragrances from glass jars decorated with ancient tiger and palm emblems. It wasn't an opulent room – but it was one decorated with a refined taste.

Blake was tapping the side of his glass with a spoon to attract everyone's attention. Next to him were Lorenzo, Binita and the Trincis. I hopped on a nearby ottoman.

"I'd like to welcome you all to this 'open morning' at the rest house," he held his arms wide. "Nothing at all formal. Just a chance to look around our new facility before our first residents arrive next week."

Looking at Lorenzo as people gathered closer, he continued,

"When Signor Conti told me that he felt he had some people to thank, I suggested we do it here. The end of one chapter, you might say, and the start of another."

"The start of several other chapters!" Lorenzo agreed emphatically, to chuckles.

Blake gestured that he should continue.

"I think that, by now, you probably know the story of why I came to be here in McLeod Ganj. All the difficulties I had trying to find out about my grandfather. Along with the most unforeseen breakthrough."

There were nods and smiles all round.

"We have just come," he continued in that soft elegant accent, indicating Binita, Serena, Sid and Mrs. Trinci, "from placing the remains of my Nonna Uma beside Padre Lorenzo. It was a … special occasion," a faraway look came into his eyes as he gazed down. "Like Blake says," he glanced to where Blake was fiddling with his cravat, "the closing of a chapter in our family history which has remained open far too long. But carrying out my Nonna's wishes brought me here to this … magical place." The luminosity in Lorenzo's hazel eyes was like the elysian light that had streamed through the forest branches earlier that morning. "It's as if she has directed me towards my own spiritual path."

As he met the eyes of each of those present, one person at a time, his words were heartfelt. "This has only been possible because of all of you. I have never felt so at home anywhere outside Italy more than in this place. Directly and indirectly, each one of you has been of the greatest support. So, before I leave McLeod Ganj, I wanted to thank you from the bottom of my heart." He brought a hand to his chest.

There was a warm ripple of appreciation from the small group, before Franc asked, "Will you be coming back?"

"Yes!" Lorenzo replied immediately. "Very soon." Shooting a glance at Binita he continued, "But when I go, I shall be taking someone with me," he reached out to take her hand.

Binita smiled self-consciously before saying, "Lorenzo has invited me to visit his family back home."

"I don't think they will believe she is real until they meet her," Lorenzo announced to some laughter. "And even then ..."

The depth of his gratitude succinctly expressed, after sharing the news that he was taking Binita to Italy, the two of them were soon mingling with others. Chatter resumed around that grand salon of rippling curtains and Indian woven carpets. Perched on the ottoman, as I gazed around taking in the large indoor plants with their lush green leaves, complemented by an array of botanical prints on the walls, it was with a feeling of completion, just like Blake had said. A circle being rounded – and at the same time, fresh possibilities.

Zahra came to me, a small dab of whipped cream on the tip of her forefinger, lifted off her scone, which I licked appreciatively. As she knelt, stroking me, I saw one of Blake's newly uniformed staff members walking towards him urgently and whispering in his ear. Blake glanced at his watch and excused himself.

He crossed the room, drawing aside the curtains. Moments later, he was showing in the Dalai Lama. As everyone realized who had arrived, conversation dramatically hushed. But His Holiness gestured that they should continue talking and not make a fuss. There were not many rooms in the world where such a request would be followed. But this was one of the very few. Chatter started up again based on a special appreciation, a particular understanding. For a moment, His Holiness looked over towards Zahra and me, his eyes twinkling.

Nearly everywhere he goes, the Dalai Lama is the center of attention, the one to whom others defer. Whether it's at home in Namgyal Monastery, delivering a speech in faraway New York, or taking part in a conference in Paris or Sydney, all eyes are focused on him. It is rare that he has the chance to simply move about, free from the attention of others.

But in this room, among people he'd known, in some cases for more than half a century, he was among friends. They may revere him as much as anyone in the outside world, but they also understand his wish not to be gawped at. To go about his day without fanfare. To freely be himself, without expectation.

Of everyone there, Blake was the most recent arrival to McLeod Ganj, but his understanding of this simple truth was instinctive. He was soon responding to His Holiness's questions about the redevelopment of the rest house. As the two of them moved in and out of the room, they discussed the roof that had been badly in need of repair in one corner of the house. The staircase requiring extensive renovation, fixing wobbly handrails and replacing many of the treads – and complemented by a spacious, new elevator . The Dalai Lama evidently knew about the building in great detail and seemed genuinely appreciative that it had been so sensitively restored.

It was a while before he approached where Serena, Sid and Mrs. Trinci were talking to Lorenzo, Binita and Marianne Ponter, Rishi playing on the carpet nearby. They opened out to include Blake and him. Taking Sid by the hand on one side and Marianne Ponter on the other, he looked at the rest of the group brightly, "They have done a good job, these ones, yes?" He gestured around the room, towards the redevelopment in general.

It was Marianne and Sid who had overseen the purchase and redevelopment of the old sanatorium, in line with Christopher Ackland's vision for a retirement home for Broke Old Bohemians. The two of them had also appointed Blake as its inaugural director.

"Blake has been showing you around?" observed Sid, as always deflecting attention away from himself.

"Oh yes!" replied His Holiness, glancing warmly towards Blake. "And he is a good person to be in charge!"

As they chuckled, he continued. "This one, I heard him before I saw him, when he came to us at Namgyal. 'Ho! Ho! Ho!'" he mimicked Blake, to further amusement.

"This is very good," he was approving. "Giving this old building new life and taking care of older people."

Some of the others in the room were drifting over to hear what the Dalai Lama was saying.

"In Western countries, the elderly are sometimes treated like outcasts. Out of sight. They can be made to feel useless. In other countries, we respect these oldies. Often, they are the ones who have given their lives to their children. So, it is a time when their children can take more care of them. This is useful, no? So that the older ones can spend whatever time that remains wisely. To extract maximum meaning from this precious human life."

As his small audience absorbed this, several nodding in agreement, His Holiness continued, "I was very happy when Blake invited me this morning. You see, in the early days after we came from Tibet in 1959, our very first home was here."

"Really?" Blake exclaimed, startled.

From the looks on faces around the room, everyone else was equally surprised.

The Dalai Lama nodded. "Even then, it was an old building. Problems with the roof. Stairs a bit unsteady," he murmured. "But we were free from attack by the Chinese. And very grateful to the Government of India for allowing us to settle here in *Dharmashala*. The rest house for spiritual pilgrims – that is what the name means. This is where we stayed until we could build Namgyal across the road."

He turned to Blake and said a few words, then the two of them were crossing the room to the door into a central hallway. The others watched, wondering if some kind of private tour was underway, before His Holiness turned, gesturing that we should join them. And so, the small gathering made its way upstairs. I was in Zahra's arms for the difficult bits, but often set down in newly appointed bedrooms to sniff at jute carpets, wicker hampers, and the pungent tang of recently polished wooden doors.

We took in the beds, with their gossamer veils of mosquito nets swaying like tranquil cocoons in the breeze. The large brass lamps with their smoky pleated shades. The large urn-like tubs on the upstairs veranda, blooming with birds of paradise. And an abundance of cane furniture waiting to be used, facing onto that most spectacular of vistas – row upon row of mountains stretching into the far distance.

Pausing to take this all in, His Holiness turned to Blake and the small group who had followed. "Very beautiful!" he said, his voice deep with feeling.

Blake nodded. For a moment he seemed to be considering whether to ask something, before the Dalai Lama looked at him directly, eyebrows raised in inquiry.

"Christopher Ackland, the artist whose fortune was used to redevelop this site, told Marianne he'd like to create a sanctuary for people like himself," he said.

His Holiness nodded. He not only knew the story – he had been part of it. Christopher had visited him, near the very end of his life, and it had been the Dalai Lama's inspiration that had set him on a trajectory that turned his death into an event of the most uplifting transcendence.

"We have been struggling with a name," continued Blake. "What to call this place? Christopher had suggested 'Sanatorium for Broke Old Bohemians'. Joking, I am sure. We don't want our residents to identify themselves as broke. Or necessarily old. Sid, Marianne and I have been discussing a moniker. A title."

The Dalai Lama followed him closely.

"We went back to Christopher's intention. His motivation

for this place was one of compassion."

For the first time ever, it seemed to me that Blake was looking uneasy, if not exactly shy. "Because of our location, directly across the road from you," he gestured. "And having just heard downstairs that you lived here for a while, I wonder if you'd mind us calling it 'Chenrezig Rest House'?"

"Of course," His Holiness agreed immediately. "Why not? The Buddha of Compassion."

Blake beamed, now unburdened, both by the need for the request, as well as the Dalai Lama's answer.

His Holiness seemed to be looking through the companions gathered around him on the upstairs balcony, and beyond the here and now, as he brought his palms to his chest in an impromptu dedication: "May the spirit of loving kindness pervade the hearts and minds of all who live and work here," he murmured simply.

Everyone responded by following him, folding their own hands as they shared and amplified his intention.

For a few moments he stood on that upstairs balcony with his eyes shut, hands in the mudra of prostration. Silhouetted against the towering splendor of the Himalayas, benevolent energy streamed from him to include not only we who were with him, but well beyond us, to everyone who might come to live and work here, now and in the future.

After a pause he murmured, "*Om mani padme hum*", the mantra of Chenrezig. Then, face lit with joy, he opened his eyes to engage the small group. "Now we go downstairs?" he asked Blake.

There was one room that especially interested him. When we reached the bottom of the brand-new enameled staircase – a great improvement, he commented, from the one he'd used in 1960 – His Holiness walked along the main passage before reaching an entrance. Leading off the left-hand side of the corridor, its door was ajar. He looked questioningly at Blake. Reaching behind him, Blake pushed it open and ushered him in.

Interlocking his fingers and bringing his hands to his chest, the Dalai Lama stepped inside, looking around the capacious chamber with childlike wonder. It was Blake's office – the one I had visited only days earlier. As His Holiness turned around, taking it all in, he seemed to be returning to a much earlier time. He was so unaffected in his interest, and the special appeal that this particular place had for him, that when he turned to Blake, the latter guessed, "This used to be your office?"

Smiling, he confirmed, before pointing at Blake. "Now … yours?"

Blake nodded.

"I can see," His Holiness gestured towards the bookshelves, filled with a variety of rare and esoteric volumes, "you have a searching mind. The wisdoms of East and West. You wish to bring together, yes?"

After a pause, glancing contemplatively from the new furniture to the wall of masks, from the colorful surrealist paintings to Blake's capacious desk, he gave Blake a twinkling smile. "Much better now than when I was here!"

The two men chuckled, the Dalai Lama moving further into the room, making his way towards the window. The small band of friends followed, relishing being in the presence of His Holiness as he explored what had evidently been such a special place for him, experiencing some of his enchantment.

His Holiness progressed steadily to the window with the banquette seat and tartan cushions, gazing towards the view beyond the window. For a while he stood, looking upon the serried ranks of mountains rising far into the distance. As Blake drew closer, he made a gesture over the Himalaya mountains into the distance. "Where we came from," he said simply.

For the first time those mountains, instead of appearing as a soaring invocation of transcendence, felt like an impenetrable barrier. An insuperable obstacle between where we were and the Dalai Lama's homeland.

"We felt safe when we got here. But it was a very long journey," he mused. "Because there was little warning, many people were not prepared with the right food. Clothes. Footwear. Too many of them died." He settled on the tartan cushions, eyes still fixed on the mountains. "In the early days, there was so much news about the destruction of our monasteries by the Red Army. The killing of monks and nuns. Much turmoil.

He sat facing in the direction of Tibet and there was a poignant silence. When he'd been forced out of Lhasa by the Chinese invaders in 1959, as well as being the spiritual leader of Tibet, His Holiness had also been its temporal leader. In his early twenties, he had tried to negotiate a political settlement with the devious Mao Tse-tung, who viewed Tibet as an easy target for invasion. And an important strategic one: the Yangtze, Mekong, Yellow and other major rivers of Asia all had their headwaters in the Tibetan plateau.

The others drew closer, settling into chairs or on the carpet nearby, understanding the extraordinary emotions he must have experienced as a young man, sitting exactly where he was right now, hearing news of his home while looking out on this same view. Mrs. Trinci took the chair closest to the Dalai Lama. In a moment, I had hopped onto her lap.

Despite the deep trauma of all he must have endured, His Holiness remained the embodiment of benevolent equanimity. Other leaders in his position may have been eaten up by anger, bitter with frustration, or cast deep into an abyss of unrelenting hopelessness. That he was none of these was something we could feel quite tangibly.

Turning towards us he said, "I did my best to visit other nations, to ask for help."

"That was the first time most of us had seen you, in the West," observed Ludwig, who had settled comfortably cross-legged on the floor nearby. "When you came on your early visits."

The Dalai Lama met his eyes.

"Sometimes, I wonder what would have happened if the Chinese hadn't invaded," continued Ludwig. "If you had stayed in Lhasa. If Tibet had remained as remote and unknown to most people as Ladakh or Sikkim."

His Holiness was nodding, having evidently contemplated this same possibility.

"Would any of us have found the *Dharma*?" Ludwig asked. "Would we know anything about Buddhism?"

The Dalai Lama shrugged. "The cause for a mind to be attracted to the *Dharma* is not outside of the mind. It is definitely not Mao Tse-tung!" His expression was wry. "If anyone has created the cause, they will definitely find the *Dharma*."

"And the cause," confirmed Blake, "is previous practice?"

"Yes, yes." His Holiness looked around us. "Today," he said, "this life, perhaps we are Tibetan or Italian. Human or cat. Male or female. But not always so."

His simple statement of impermanence and karma was accompanied by transmission at a different level, so it felt that he was not so much repeating a Buddhist teaching as reminding us of something we already knew. Reconnecting us to a basic truth about ourselves that we seldom perceived, wrapped up as we were in the immediate drama of this life, here and now.

His Holiness continued, "If you live next door to a highly realized lama, and you have no causes in your mindstream to be inclined to the *Dharma*, you will always see the lama as just an ordinary person. But even if you live in the most remote place on earth, if you have created the cause, the *Dharma* will definitely appear to you. Perhaps in a book. Or someone you meet. That book or person will inspire you, and encourage you to continue. The more we nourish our practice, the stronger it becomes, lifetime after lifetime."

The claw of attraction, dear reader.

It was only when he turned back from the view outside,

that he caught sight of what had attracted me to this spot on my previous visit – the stone casket with its intricate carvings.

"Oh!" he exclaimed appreciatively, reaching out to touch it, before looking directly at Blake. "This is very old?"

"From Gandhara," confirmed Blake.

Hands still placed on the smooth curved sides of the casket, His Holiness closed his eyes as if to divine its extraordinary purpose.

"From a very special time and place," he spoke after a pause, his voice resonant with feeling. "East and West," he flashed Blake a look of warm appreciation, reprising his previous remark.

Blake nodded.

"Twenty-five hundred years ago," the Dalai Lama lifted his hands from the stone, while still holding it with an expression of great reverence. "Gandhara," he looked up at us, "was an ancient place, west of here. Conquered by Alexander the Great. Several Indo-Greek kings became Buddhist. The first encounter with Buddhism by Westerners in about 300BCE. They even had coins with the eight-spoked wheel on them."

"I had no idea!" Mrs. Trinci confessed. "I thought Buddhism only came to the West when you did!"

His Holiness burst out laughing before meeting the eyes of Zahra, who was sitting on the carpet. He touched the banquette cushion, inviting her to sit next to him.

In an instant, Zahra had got up and hurried to his side where they embraced briefly. The Dalai Lama had known her since she'd been born, having been a family friend for decades.

This was the first time he'd seen her since her return from Britain. No longer a child, she sat next to him now as a poised and beautiful young woman.

"There are many influences, relationships not always apparent, in any one moment," His Holiness continued. And was it my imagination, or did he glance briefly from Zahra to me as he spoke? "The influence of West on East. East on West. The *Dharma*, constantly moving, sometimes dramatically, sometimes in more subtle but profound ways. Buddha himself compared it to a golden yoke floating on the surface of a huge deep ocean in his *Sutra Containing the Excellent*, constantly carried by the winds this way and that. From Nepal, where Shakyamuni was born, to present day India. Through the influence of Ashoka the Great throughout Asia. The winds took the *Dharma* from India to Tibet, to China and countries in the South East. More recently from Tibet to the West. Wherever beings have minds to perceive it, the *Dharma* appears."

"So, are you saying," asked Zahra beside him, marveling not only at the vision he had been describing, but also at its personal significance, "that someone whose mind may perhaps have been that of a Greek in the time of Gandhara and a Tibetan in a later time and now, maybe, a Westerner – such a being's mind helps cause the *Dharma* to appear?"

"Of course!" His Holiness nodded. "Buddha, *Dharma* and *Sangha*. All arise from mind."

"And perhaps some of us have been on this journey lasting millennia together?"

"All are interconnected," he confirmed.

As he did, he shifted in his seat to create more space for Zahra. Looking down, he noticed a swatch of white fur stuck to his red robe. In an instant he looked at me, scraping the fur off his robe with ease of practice and holding it up to Blake.

"She has already been here?" he asked.

"Two days ago," the other confirmed. "She went directly to where you are now," he nodded. "And sat there."

His Holiness chortled, shoulders shaking with laughter. "You see!" he handed the fur to Zahra ceremoniously. "We are all interconnected."

While amusement rippled around the room, Serena spoke. "None of what's happened here today would have been possible without HHC. She was the one, after all, who found the marker for Luna's grave under the shrubs in Mum's garden. And who discovered Lorenzo at The Himalaya Book Café, and again at Geshe Wangpo's class in the temple."

As she spoke, the Dalai Lama followed the sequence of events with amused interest, looking from Mrs. Trinci to Lorenzo, who were agreeing.

"If it hadn't been for her antics that night," continued Serena, "Sam would never have admired Lorenzo's pen, Lorenzo would never have given it to him, and Binita would never have made the crucial connection. So, you see?" she shrugged, arms held out expansively.

"It all comes back to HHC!" Franc emphasized her message.

"Exactly!" Mrs. Trinci's eyelids fluttered, as she stroked me effusively. "The Most Beautiful Creature That Ever Lived!"

"I rejoice for all who see His Holiness's Cat as this creature of great love and wisdom," the Dalai Lama responded to Serena's account. "Not all who see her have the same view."

"I know!" Franc said with feeling. "Some of the customers down at the café are appalling. We had the President of some Cat Fancier's Association wanting to euthanize her because of how she walks."

"Like this," His Holiness nodded, utterly unsurprised. "Just as the *Dharma* can only arise in the minds of those who have the karma for it," he turned to Zahra, lifting her hand into his own, "it is the same with all other things. The beauty you see in the world is coming from you – from your past virtue. If you experience peace of heart, it is because of your mind, your virtuous karma."

Outside, the sun had risen and a glorious Himalayan morning streamed through the open windows, vibrant with promise.

"So, how wonderful is it," continued the Dalai Lama, "when we find ourselves among a group of old friends we have known for many years? Decades? People with whom we've been on this journey together, and will continue to be?"

Every word he spoke touched the hearts of those present so powerfully that we were lifted quite beyond our usual preoccupations to a more sublime and timeless reality. One we sensed to be more important and enduring than any other.

"If we have created precious bonds with one another, we will continue to be interconnected in the future. We will never get lost, but help by supporting each other on our journey to enlightenment, because we are creating the causes for that to happen."

Above me, Mrs. Trinci was dabbing her eyes as His Holiness spoke.

"A good heart," he brought his right hand to his chest. "A good mind. Taking refuge in the Buddha, the *Dharma* and also …" he gestured about the room, "the *Sangha*. Our fellow practitioners. *These* are true causes of happiness, now and in the future."

As we all sat, minds enjoined completely with his, we were as one.

"How fortunate are we?" concluded His Holiness.

How fortunate indeed! And if you, too, dear reader, have listened attentively with us over the years at Geshe Wangpo's Tuesday evening classes, eavesdropped on meaningful conversations at The Himalaya Book Café, spent evenings in the semidarkness of the balcony at The Downward Dog School of Yoga, or attended transmissions with Yogi Tarchin, then you are one of us. Part of our circle. Journeying together on the path to enlightenment, which becomes a self-fulfilling prophecy the more we create the causes for its inevitable blossoming. His Holiness's transcendent benediction includes you too!

EPILOGUE

"GIVEN THAT THIS WAS YOUR HOME LONG BEFORE WE MOVED in," Blake spoke after a while, "and at such an important time of your life, would you like a few moments here alone?"

The Dalai Lama regarded him appreciatively for a few moments, before giving an almost imperceptible nod.

Quietly, the others got up and left the room. For a time His Holiness stood, gazing out over the lawn and the forest to the far blue mountains. Folding palms at his heart and whispering silent mantras, I wondered how attainable a return to Lhasa may have seemed when he'd first arrived in this place. Had he hoped for a change of heart on the part of Mao Tse-tung, allowing him to return home, and for Tibet to enjoy the limited autonomy he so fervently sought? Or had he already known that such a dream was unattainable? Would he ever have thought that, sixty years later, he'd find himself in this same room, looking at this same view, with the prospect of a return more distant than ever?

And what would have happened if he *had* been able to return home? Would I have been born as a cat in Tibet and somehow found my way to the windowsill of his room, high in the Potala Palace overlooking Lhasa? Or would I have been left to die inside a scrunched-up newspaper on the streets of Delhi? Would all those Western students have been reborn as Tibetans, and would the *Dharma* have continued to be practiced in seclusion, behind the most formidable range of mountains on earth?

For a moment, I reached both front paws before me and stretched in an extravagant sun salutation. The Dalai Lama gazed at me with a smile, as he took in my high bushy tail, quivering legs and – longer than they should have been – my exposed talons.

"Are you revealing the claw of attraction, my little Snow Lion?" he murmured, bending to scoop me into his arms as he turned again to the window.

In an instant, I recalled the social media influencers in their impossibly large pink vehicle. How the Dalai Lama had quickly corrected their idea of wanting him to reveal magical forces to make their dreams come true, creating wealth, romance and other worldly attainments. How he had, instead, explained the importance of cultivating that true source of happiness – the mind of enlightenment. As we gazed into the distance, I reflected on the intriguing insights and powerful practices I had come to learn since then about *bodhichitta* and *shunyata.*

How I had discovered that Mrs. Trinci added *bodhichitta* motivation as her special ingredient to every cake she baked and every meal she prepared. By weaving *bodhichitta* – the wish to attain enlightenment for the sake of every living being – into everyday actions, especially those she engaged in with such bountiful fervor, she was deliberately shifting the focus of her attention from self to other. Was it any surprise that, over the years, her volatile nature had become imbued with an equally open-hearted state of deep wellbeing?

From Serena, in her conversation with a despairing Binita, I had learned the value of *bodhichitta* as a protective amulet. A mental talisman to be prized. And whether one chose *bodhichitta*, gratitude or some other authentic treasure, what a wonder to discover the truth that whatever we place in front of our mind, it faithfully reflects. As we think, so we become.

Not everyone who practices loving kindness appears that way, as our Scottish visitor Bill had demonstrated with such consummate peevishness. He completely lacked the ability to emote sweetness and light. But trudging through the mean streets of his city into the early hours of the morning, to take care of the homeless, was a mission to which he had devoted his life. Some *bodhisattvas* are of the jellybean variety, their forbidding exterior concealing the purest of hearts.

Yogi Tarchin had explained *shunyata,* that other wing of enlightenment, to Heidi, outlining how everything in the world – you and I included – is dependent on factors other than themselves. Being dependent on parts, causes and mental perceptions – elements which are constantly changing – means that there is no permanent reality to anything. Plankton are ingested by tuna fish. Tuna fish get turned into cat food. Cat food, after consumption, inevitably finds its way into a spot in the garden, perhaps under a bush, after which it may find fresh manifestation as a beautiful rose. All is in a state of becoming, of change – which is why enlightenment is possible. If we were stuck with the permanent version of who we are right now, all we could expect in the future is more of the same. By imbuing our consciousness with the positive causes for future positive effects, transformation is not simply possible, but inevitable.

Geshe Wangpo had been commanding in his explanation of how exactly to turbocharge our trajectory. By deliberately recollecting *shunyata* – the ultimate nature of reality – when undertaking positive actions of body, speech and mind, we ensure that the effects of those actions ripen in this ultimate reality, rather than in our usual experience of *samsara*. We are, in a way, creating a meritorious bank account that propels us to enlightenment. If ever there was a precious purpose for the law of attraction, dear reader, this was it!

One evening on the balcony of The Downward Dog School of Yoga, Ludo had eloquently answered Ricardo's question about how to focus on both *bodhichitta* and *shunyata*. By familiarizing ourselves with the motivation of bodhichitta so deeply that it moves from an object of the mind to a state of heart, authentic and spontaneous, as habitual perhaps as wearing a pair of sunglasses, then whenever we recollect *shunyata* with such a mind, we are practicing *bodhichitta* also.

It was Blake Ballantyne, our ebullient newcomer, who

had offered the shortest encapsulation of *shunyata* in the form of The Heart Sutra mantra, the recitation of which creates the most incalculable benefits: *Tadyatha om gaté gaté paragaté parasamgaté bodhi svaha.*

With a mind ever alert to transcendent treasures, not to mention intriguing interconnection, it was Blake who had also revealed how East and West had influenced each other, long before even the Common Era. How much had Hellenistic Greek art influenced that of Asia, especially in the way Buddha is depicted? How much had Shakyamuni Buddha's thoughts influenced that of Greek philosophers, and through them, Western philosophy? Much more than we had ever dreamed.

Sid had explained interconnection in a much more personal sense: why we are drawn to certain people for reasons we can't explain. How sentient beings of all kinds come into our lives, because of karmic bonds shared from previous lifetimes. What's more, in shaping our consciousness and our future destiny, how intriguing it is that we are influenced not only by beings we know personally, but even by those we may not know, but to whom we open our hearts and minds. Teachers, leaders, those we read about – the more we resonate with them, the more we empower the likelihood of our future closeness.

His Holiness had emphasized the importance of patiently nourishing our practice. *Bodhichitta* and *shunyata*, like all other jewels of the *Dharma*, were not simply to be studied and intellectually admired, but were to be worn. Practiced and used as agents of change.

In our journey together, the Dalai Lama had also warmly

acknowledged the value of our fellow travelers: the *Sangha*. Beings with whom we had shared our journey of countless incarnations. Who could tell how many rooms we had sat in together? Meals we had shared? Teachings we had attended in one another's company?

Held at His Holiness's shoulder that morning, gazing into the distance, suddenly it didn't seem to matter so much whether we were here together, instead of at the Potala Palace. From a more panoramic perspective, the circumstances of one lifetime, even the country in which that life was lived, became much less important than the purpose to which that life was put.

I purred my gratitude for this moment, here and now, and my closeness to this extraordinary being, all that was of ultimate importance. Whether one lives in Lhasa or McLeod Ganj – or come to that, London or Los Angeles, Munich or Melbourne – is of absolutely no consequence. Whether we are cat or human, rich or poor, young or old, what matters is that we continue in the company of our fellow travelers on our journey of transcendence.

Bountiful waves of benevolence flowed from the heart of His Holiness, with a power as palpable as the joy and gratitude of my own deepening purr. How lucky I am to be the Dalai Lama's Cat! And how fortunate, dear readers, that our minds are drawn together! In our adventures, we have explored a subject of wisdom so high that there is none higher – *shunyata*. A motivation so great that there is none greater – *bodhichitta*.

From this peak of ultimate wisdom and altruism, may

waves of loving kindness extend from each one of us through the ten directions with unstoppable energy and light, touching the hearts and minds of all sentient beings and leading them to a state of infinite bliss.

> *May all beings have happiness and the true causes of happiness.*
> *May all beings be free from suffering and the true causes of suffering.*
> *May all beings never be parted from the happiness that is beyond suffering, great nirvana liberation.*
> *May all beings abide in peace and equanimity, their minds free from attachment, aversion and free from ignorance.*

DEDICATION

Through reading, thinking and meditating

And the actions flowing from these,

May anyone who encounters this book

Purify all negative karmas and accumulate infinite virtue.

Blossoming under the guidance of precious teachers,

May we all have long life, good health and profound wellbeing.

By letting go of our very selves,

May we taste the exalted joy of enlightenment.

Then may we, as Buddhas,

Support all sentient beings throughout universal space.

By manifesting spontaneously and effortlessly in myriad forms

May we help those who experience their selves as separate and suffering

Quickly to realize their own Buddha nature,

So that all may abide in the sublime state

Of radiant compassion and boundless wisdom,

Non-dual, great bliss and shunyata.

ABOUT THE AUTHOR

DAVID MICHIE IS THE INTERNATIONALLY BESTSELLING AUTHOR of *The Dalai Lama's Cat* series, *The Magician of Lhasa*, *The Secret Mantra, Instant Karma: The day it happened* and other books including the non-fiction titles *Buddhism for Busy People, Buddhism for Pet Lovers, Mindfulness is Better than Chocolate* and *Hurry Up and Meditate.*

In 2015, he established Mindful Safaris to Africa, combining wildlife viewing and meditation sessions in journeys to unexplored places, outer and inner.

For more about his work go to: *https://davidmichie.com/*

You can sign up for his regular newsletter at: *https://davidmichie.substack.com/*

Printed in Great Britain
by Amazon

53980072R00142